Connections

R. L. MOSZ

Edited by Alison Jack, www.alisonjack-editor.co.uk, Twitter @AlisonEditor1
Cover art by Elizabeth Daniel
Cover, Interior Design by Woven Red Author Services, www.WovenRed.ca

Connections/R.L. Mosz—1st edition
ISBN print book: 978-0-9600769-0-1

For Mary

Contents

Golden Boy

"Hey, Nina! Like my new car?" Tony waved to me from across the road where he had parked in front of my sister's coffee shop, The Green Earth. His father had recently bought him a used sky-blue convertible for his high-school graduation present.

Clutching an armload of schoolbooks against my side, I noted beautiful eighteen-year-old Jennifer next to him in the passenger's seat and my fourteen-year-old heart sank. Her long, sun-streaked hair shone like gold. With a disappointed sigh, I trudged across the street to see his new car—not that it interested me. Vehicles in general bored me senseless, but I had been enamored with Tony since the first grade.

"Yeah, it's nice." I attempted a small smile.

"Nice?" He grinned boyishly, his handsome face a squint. "It's beeeautiful!" To my chagrin, he reached out and patted me on the top of the head like I was a puppy dog. "See ya!" With that, he turned the key in the ignition and peeled away, the two of them soon lost in a cloud of dust.

"Now what's the matter?" my sister Susanna demanded moments later after I'd seated myself at a table in her coffee shop. She surveyed me critically, yet not without a trace of sisterly affection.

"Nothing." I glowered and sighed.

"Is that all you can ever say? You know, you shouldn't wear your hair like that. Why do you always put a bobby pin in the side?" Wrenching the pin out of my dark hair, she flung it savagely into a nearby trash bin. "It makes you look like a dork." She attempted to fluff up my hair so it didn't lie as flat across the top of my head.

"Gee, thanks." Not only did I feel like a dork, apparently I looked like one, too.

My second-to-the-oldest sister, Brooklyn, moved in closer, her arms around a tub of dirty dishes that she had cleared from a nearby table. "I saw you talking to Tony out front," she informed me with a perturbed smile.

Susanna immediately zeroed in with interest. "Tony? Oh, so that's it!" She laughed, anxious as usual to interfere. "He's too old for you. Besides, you're too young to be interested in a boy." She studied me with an air of critical enjoyment.

"I'm not interested in him!" It was impossible to keep a secret of any kind while living in a small town with five sisters.

"He's nice looking, and intelligent, too," Brooklyn remarked, sensitive to the impossibility of my infatuation, yet supportive all the same. "Wasn't he awarded a full scholarship to Brown University?" Introverted and intellectual, she had just graduated from college with honors herself as an English major. "He's a talented cellist, too."

"He's also Polish," Susanna added, accepting the tray of dishes from her sister. "Grandma would like that. And his father owns The Little Shepherdess." We were also of Polish descent and the wheels in her mind were obviously turning. The Little Shepherdess, a five-star restaurant, served only Polish cuisine and was the priciest establishment in town. "Do you think he'd be interested in Celeste?" Susanna pondered, turning to Brooklyn while ignoring my discomfiture.

My sister Celeste was three years older than I and attended the other high school in town. She and Tony barely knew each other. I arose from my chair and disappeared behind the swinging doors to clean the kitchen.

൞·ൟ

Two weeks later, I ended up helping out at Tony's graduation party at the Farmdale Community Center where the food was being catered by my sister's restaurant.

Jennifer was there and seemed permanently fixed at Tony's side. She wore a sleeveless silver dress and her hair fell in a shiny sheet to her waist. I'd dressed in a vain attempt to appear older, but alongside Jennifer, I felt plagued with insecurities about my looks. I was at that awkward adolescent age, and no matter what I did with my appearance, I still looked fourteen.

"Tony, play for us!" His father, Stanley, clapped his hands together and pulled Tony's cello from against the wall. I'd heard Stanley had initially hoped Tony would become a professional musician, having already invested a small fortune into a music career for his son. However, the decision regarding Tony's intention to attend medical school had not exactly been a crushing blow.

"Yes, Tony! Play that piece you performed last month at the amphitheater!" his aunt Bess exclaimed as she motioned the guests into nearby chairs.

I glanced lethargically at Tony as I arranged platters of hors d'oeuvres along the tables set out for the milling crowd, secretly disgruntled over my serf-like status. My father, not unlike Tony's, possessed an obsessive work ethic and had his children constantly helping out at his bookstore and Susanna's coffee shop.

To my surprise, Tony's normally compliant, cheerful expression appeared rather dour. He shook his head and leaned closer to his father, but I caught the words.

"Dad, I don't really feel like playing tonight."

"Oh, c'mon, Tony," his father insisted as he waved his son's awkwardness away without as much as a second thought. "Everyone! Gather round and grab a chair!"

With a trace of reluctance, Tony accepted the cello. He played beautifully, neatly capturing the subtle nuances of the piece. Stanley stood by with his arms folded across his chest and beamed proudly. The music brought tears to people's eyes, but from where I was standing, I had a clear view of Tony's profile. It dawned on me that mine was not the only family with problems. Tony was not a happy boy that night.

ଓ·୪

"How is Tony doing?" I asked Stanley bashfully months later while dining with my family at The Little Shepherdess to celebrate my grandmother's birthday.

"Great! He made the dean's list!" Stanley smiled and handed us our menus. Although their facial features were similar, the resemblance between father and son ended there. Stanley's squat stature proved a marked contrast to that of his tall and graceful son. Tony most resembled his beautiful deceased mother. Stanley's sister, Bess, had stepped in years earlier to fill the void. Stanley and Bess were first generation immigrants from Poland and devout Catholics, unlike my family, who had left the Church before I was born.

"Is he coming home for Christmas?" I pressed, anxious to see him again despite the fact that the chasm between us had continued to deepen. I was fifteen now and he was a college boy a thousand miles away. However, he and Jennifer had parted ways. I often saw her around town with a new boyfriend.

"The day after tomorrow, as a matter of fact!" Stanley grinned and hurried away, anxious to get back to the other customers in the crowded dining room.

My mother regarded me irritably for bothering the host. Susanna leaned closer to Celeste and began to whisper. Brooklyn smiled sympathetically, and my brothers, Matthew and Jimmy, laughed over my schoolgirl crush. My younger sisters, Andrea and Jeanette, colored their menus, but Andrea looked up momentarily.

"I know Tony's cousin. She's in my class. She said Tony has a new girlfriend whose father is the president of the university."

Snatching my menu, I pretended to be interested in the impressive list of entrees while feeling like I was suffering from the world's most hopeless case of unrequited love.

℘·℘

Tony came home for Christmas, and many more times after that. He graduated from college the year I graduated high school, seeming more attractive, brilliant, and self-assured with each appearance back in town. His father could barely contain his pride. It burst out at every opportunity. My father virtually ignored me and the contrast was difficult to overcome. Tony always had a wave and a smile for me when we passed on the street, but with every encounter, I sensed his interest diminishing. By now I was too old to be patted on top of the head.

One Thanksgiving holiday when I was eighteen, I spied Tony and his family exiting their car in front of the Church to attend Sunday Mass together. I watched from across the street while holding a cup of coffee and a pastry. Despite my family's prejudice against organized religion, I suddenly wished we were still Catholic and celebrating Mass together. As I sipped my coffee on the deserted street corner, I felt like an orphan.

℘·℘

The following summer, Tony did not come home. I thought

little about it because his image no longer occupied my thoughts like it had in years past. Forced to work my way through college, I'd dropped out after a year and worked several jobs instead.

One morning, completely on a whim, I slipped into St. Mary's. It surprised me to discover so many people there at such an early hour. The following Easter, I became a Catholic.

Now attending Mass every week, I began spotting Stanley, Aunt Bess, and the rest of the Kolinski clan filing into the church. Stanley seemed surprised to see me, but nonetheless, we struck up a friendship. Tony had been accepted into Harvard to earn a medical degree, but his father had uncharacteristically ceased to brag about the exploits of his genius son.

I realized why when Tony returned home for Christmas. He had changed dramatically, but not for the better. He still appeared well-liked and attractive, but in a slightly twisted, unnerving sort of way. The formerly health-conscious medical student now smoked and had surrounded himself with an entourage of new friends, none of whom struck me as being particularly studious.

Tony laughed a lot. In fact, he laughed too much.

While he was standing on a street corner one afternoon with his friends, I managed to get a word in edgewise and informed Tony that I had become a Catholic. Dragging hard on his cigarette, he could not have appeared more bored with the revelation.

"Now why in the world would you want to do that to yourself?" he said, peering deeply into my eyes.

಄·಄

"How's Tony doing these days?" I asked Stanley one afternoon a year later as he purchased a few items for his restaurant. In addition to my full-time job, I was also employed part-time at the local grocery. My latest goal was to save up for a down payment on the abandoned Monforton place outside of town. I planned to become a farmer.

Stanley set his mouth in a grim line. "How should I know?" He shook his head. "He's never there when I call."

"He's probably busy," I replied. "He must have a lot of studying to do."

Stanley scowled, appearing older under the fluorescent lighting. "Then why are there always people laughing... music... noise... when I do manage to reach him?" Clasping his packages to his chest, he cast me a look of a man deserted in his old age and headed for the exit. After only a few steps, however, he turned around again and his eyes searched mine. "Nina, if he comes home for Thanksgiving... maybe the two of you could go out someplace?"

I almost laughed. His son was even less interested in me now than he had been when I was fourteen, if that were possible; and besides, I'd long since discarded the notion of ever having been in love with him. Susanna's insights had proven correct: at fourteen, I'd been too young to fall in love.

"Well, we'll see. Have a nice day, Stanley."

He made his way out the door, his head held low in sorrow. There was a stoop to his walk, as if a weight had settled upon him. I turned back to arranging the bills in the cash drawer, my smile turning to a grimace.

৪০·৫৪

Tony did come home for Thanksgiving, but he didn't need a date after all. He brought one with him. He showed up at Susanna's coffee shop one afternoon with his entourage of friends and his new girlfriend.

Surveying her critically from across the room, I felt a twinge of sympathy for poor old Stanley. She was the sort of girl you'd never want your son to end up dating. Thin and heavily made up, she wore a perpetual look of self-conceit and whined nonstop about everything in sight.

It seemed as though the group lived strictly to play. They laughed too much, talked too loud, and were a disruption to everyone else in the room.

Susanna grew furious. "I ought to throw your friend out of here," she remarked as her eyes traveled to Tony's table for the fifth time in less than a minute. "He's really turned out to be an inconsiderate jerk. He'll make a great doctor," she added angrily, her bad mood now in full swing.

"He's not my friend," I replied. I hated working for her, but needed the money.

Susanna pushed a strand of brown hair back from her face while bussing a table. "I hear he never lifts a finger to help his father at that restaurant any longer. Apparently, he considers menial work beneath him now." With a final withering look at her unwelcome customers, she turned back to the kitchen to pull some pastries from the oven.

I glanced back at Tony and recalled how he used to wait tables for his father at The Little Shepherdess and maintain a perfect grade point average in high school. I hoped when he did graduate and become a doctor that he'd practice in another town, and we'd finally be rid of him forever.

80·CB

"Did you hear about Tony Kolinski?" my sister Andrea asked a month later. Christmas was three days away.

"No," I responded flatly. Andrea suffered from a penchant for gossip.

"I heard from his cousin that he dropped out of medical school. His father is devastated."

I shook my head and wondered how much money Stanley had shelled out for all that wasted education. My father had refused to pay for my schooling. "What's he doing if he's no longer at the university?"

"Evidently he got a great job with a friend of his. He just bought himself a new car and rented a garden apartment in New York."

"What's the job?" I asked.

Andrea shrugged. "I'm not sure. I think it's in marketing or something. His friend's father lined it up for him."

ᛞ·ᛞ

The next time Tony showed up in town, he was driving a car that would have easily paid the down payment on the Monforton place several times over. I surveyed the sleek, shiny green sports car resentfully as I stood outside the local grocery. I'd been saving for years to buy the old farm while Tony could afford anything he wanted, and he hardly seemed to be working that much. From what I'd heard, he was constantly vacationing with friends. I felt tired just standing on the curb after my long shift in the grocery.

"Hey, Nina! Like my new car?" Tony smiled as he slid into the driver's seat, his silly girlfriend close behind him. It seemed a miracle that the two of them were still together, but then, they did have a lot in common.

"I hate it!" I shouted as they pulled away from the curb. They didn't hear me or care as Tony gunned the engine and the car careened down the street.

ᛞ·ᛞ

"He doesn't go to church anymore," Stanley confided as he huddled over his cup of coffee. "He's been living with that... that girl!"

We were sitting in a window booth at Susanna's coffee shop. "Well, that probably won't last." My words sounded hollow and untrue. "And a lot of people leave the Church for a while. It's probably just a stage."

Stanley shook his head. There were deep worry lines etched into his features. His hair was completely gray.

"The last time he was here, I hardly saw him. He doesn't care about his family anymore. We're just a joke to him now." He looked up from his coffee. "Does he still talk to you?"

"No." It was my turn to shake my head. I placed my hand over Stanley's callused one. "At least he's working. He seems to be a big success anyway."

Stanley's expression grew angry. "A success? He's going to end up in prison! Marketing? Pah!"

‽·⁎

A month later, I made an offer on the Monforton place. Lila Monforton, now advanced in age, took pity on me and accepted it. Another bid was submitted days later for twice my amount by an investor from out of town, but we'd already signed the papers. I'd snatched the place up just in time.

After Mass the following Sunday, I caught up with Bess to ask after Stanley. I wanted to tell him about my good fortune.

"He's not here, Nina." Her expression appeared strained. "He's in New York. Tony's been arrested."

"Arrested?" I grew shocked. "For what?"

"Drugs." Bess leaned closer. "He's been arrested for dealing drugs. They found a load of hashish in his garage."

"How terrible!"

"Yes." She nodded. "It's really terrible."

‽·⁎

After Tony was convicted and sentenced to ten years in prison, Stanley returned from New York a broken man. Farmdale's former golden boy was now incarcerated, and that was the last anyone heard about Tony for a long time.

The years passed uneventfully. I attempted to renovate the old farm, but it required resources and skills I lacked. Instead, I worked a stream of jobs to maintain the place.

People were moving in from the urban areas close by and I had many offers on my unfarmed farm, which I could easily have unloaded at any time for a handsome profit, but my dream of becoming a farmer stayed as strong as ever.

In addition to my renovation troubles, a new problem emerged. After the slow dissolution of my schoolgirl crush on Tony, I seemed unable to find a suitable match for myself. By now all five of my sisters were married and having children.

There were two parishes in Farmdale, and I began attending the more traditional St. Jude's. I never dined at The Little Shepherdess, so I rarely saw Stanley, but one day, I bumped into him on my lunch hour as I was leaving the post office.

"Hi, Stanley."

He turned to face me, his expression grim. "Oh, hi, Nina."

I was surprised to discover how frail he appeared. His restaurant was a booming business, but there was no trace of happiness in his expression.

"How have you been?"

He shrugged. "All right."

I hesitated. "How's Tony?"

"Terrible."

"Oh." My breath caught in my throat. "I'm sorry to hear that."

"Yeah, well." He shrugged again. "I blame myself—I ruined him."

"That's not true," I replied. Stanley's ashen features alarmed me. "You were a great father to him. My father didn't pay any attention to me," I added, hoping to boost his spirits.

"Same thing."

"What?" I wondered if he might be getting a touch of senile.

"I was too proud of him. Your father wasn't proud of you at all. It's the same thing."

He turned away and vanished into the crowd.

&·&

"Why don't you like Casey?" Susanna asked as she rolled out a slab of croissant dough. I had just broken the news to her that I wasn't interested in the recent date she'd set up for me with her husband Larry's friend.

I sighed. "Oh, you know. He's a bit old for me. Did you know that he drinks a lot? I think he's an alcoholic."

"Well, he's a farmer," my sister said, as if that somehow mitigated the alcohol problem. "Casey could fix up that dump you live in. And he's crazy about you."

"He's not as crazy about me as he is his bottle."

"Look, Nina, don't ask me to try and help you out anymore. Don't expect Larry to fix your leaky faucets and frayed wires. From now on, you're on your own." She slammed the rolling pin down on the wooden table and cast me a stern look as she prepared to fold the dough.

"I never asked you to do that," I replied doggedly. It always seemed with my family that we were on a revolving stage.

Travis, the busboy, appeared. "Susanna, I have the front all cleaned up," he informed her as he flashed me a friendly smile. "Hi, Nina."

"Hi." I sighed. He was too young. It was nearly time to go unload pallets at the emporium for eight hours.

"Hey, did you hear the big news?" Travis asked. "Remember that guy… the son of the man who owns The Little Shepherdess?"

Susanna began rolling the dough out again. "You mean the one who ended up in the penitentiary?"

I studied Travis with interest. "Tony Kolinski?"

"Yeah, that's who I mean. I heard he just got out of prison. They knocked two years off for good behavior." Travis popped a chocolate cookie into his mouth.

"Is he coming back to Farmdale?" I asked. It was hard to believe that eight years had already passed.

Travis nodded. "Uh-huh. His father left yesterday to go get him."

☙ · ❧

In the ensuing weeks, I kept a sharp eye out for the former golden boy. I spied a few members of the Kolinski family, but Tony was never with them. I wondered if he had already relocated, perhaps to live with relatives in another state. One could hardly blame the man if he had, considering the small town of prying eyes, including my own.

One day at the coffee shop, the head waitress, Gwen, broached the subject. We were sitting with two other employees and my sister Jeanette.

"I heard his brain is totally fried," Gwen pronounced dramatically, her beautiful eyes sweeping the table as she reveled in our shocked expressions. "My neighbor said she went to school with him, and he couldn't even remember who she was. Isn't that awful?"

"That's terrible," Jeanette admitted as she sipped her tea.

"Maybe he didn't remember her because it's been so long," I muttered, as tired of Gwen as I was of the men people kept suggesting I date. She constantly passed untrue information along.

Gwen shook her head. "Well, ask anyone who's seen him. Remember how charming and outgoing he used to be? He's just the opposite now. He never smiles or talks anymore. It's because he damaged his brain taking all those drugs. He looks dreadful, too. He's really aged."

"He spent a lot of years locked up," Jeannette mused. "That prison he was in is one of the worst ones, too. I heard that from a friend whose brother-in-law worked there as a guard."

"Well, what's he doing?" I asked, anxious to get off the subject of the penitentiary. I knew Tony wasn't working with his father at the restaurant. No one I knew had seen him there.

"That's just it," Gwen responded, as always completely in the know. "He can't even wait tables any longer. He has to work on his uncle's farm… shoveling manure!"

He was working on his uncle's farm. That was close by The Dump, as the town had aptly named the old Monforton place. We were actually neighbors.

ଔ·ଓ

I finally saw him a month later. Heading down Hemlock Road in my old Dodge, I spotted him walking up ahead in the noonday sun. His lanky form and relaxed walk were unmistakable, even from a distance.

As my car drew nearer, I tensed. Finding myself descending into an immature state of panic, I passed by on the road, pretending not to see him. I glanced in my rearview mirror and sighed with relief. He had failed to recognize me, instead staring into the distance at the hills as he walked along.

The scene replayed in my mind all day, and later that night, I found myself unable to sleep. Why hadn't I stopped and offered him a ride? It had to have been ninety-five degrees at the time; it was still an uncomfortably warm, humid night. All the years he'd spent in prison, I'd never visited or written him once.

Ruminating over the situation, I lay awake as the hours ticked away until morning.

ଔ·ଓ

I didn't see him again until autumn. The entire scenario repeated itself as I drove down Hemlock Road in my Dodge, spying him as he walked up ahead. This time his figure was framed by canopies of orange and gold.

As I slowed to a stop, my heart pounded with a mixture of curiosity and dread. I looked out at him.

"Hi, Tony. Can I offer you a ride?"

He glanced at me in surprise. "Hi, Nina. All right, and thanks."

He remembered me.

Tony climbed into the passenger's seat and crowded his long legs in the narrow space. With a quick smile, he reached for the lever to adjust the seat.

"It's broken," I informed him. "Like just about everything else in this car."

"Oh." He nodded.

As usual, Gwen had been way off. He looked older, but still very attractive. His face appeared freckled and tanned from the sun. I felt tremendously relieved.

"How have you been, Nina?"

"Okay." A silenced followed and I cleared my throat. "I was really sorry to hear what happened to you eight years ago. And I'm sorry I never bothered to write. I'm glad you're home."

He glanced away. That day he said very little. After sliding out at his destination, he turned to wave. Deep in his eyes, I saw a quality of circumspection that startled me.

After that afternoon, I saw him more often, occasionally spotting him at the early morning daily Mass. One afternoon, I encountered him at the library with an armload of books. I glanced at the top book's cover—*Les Misérables*.

"It's a great story," he said, his expression almost shy.

"I've never read it. What does the title mean?"

"The Miserable Ones."

"Oh." I tried to think up something to say. Silence loomed instead.

He didn't seem to mind. "That old Monforton place is worth a fortune now," he said at last. "You were smart to save up for so long to buy it. Are you planning to sell?"

Despite its rundown aspect, my property had increased markedly in value during the past few years. I shook my head.

"I didn't buy it to make a killing, although it did nearly kill me to buy it."

He laughed. "Just want to live there, then?"

"Yeah. I just like living there. Need a ride?" I asked.

"That would be great. I've walked a lot today."

As we settled into the car and he tucked in his long legs, he turned to study me a moment. "You need a truck, Nina. Farmers are supposed to drive trucks."

I nodded. "I can't afford one. I'm too poor to be a farmer."

€&#x7; C&#x7;

After that, Tony stopped by my farm to help out with an occasional chore. Initially, I was reluctant to accept the help, but soon felt at ease with the situation. He didn't offer his assistance too often, and I felt no strings attached to the favors.

One afternoon, after he'd finished hanging a door, I offered to pay him something. He waved me away and wiped his sensitively sculpted hands against his faded jeans. I wondered if he ever played the cello any longer.

"Don't worry about it," he insisted. "It's not a big deal."

"I could afford to play you something."

He shook his head. "No, I don't want anything." He settled himself on the edge of the porch to rest a moment and gazed across the open fields that traveled up to the distant mountains. The place enjoyed a spectacular view.

"I had this friend," I began reluctantly. "Actually, he's your neighbor... Casey Roundtree."

"I know Casey." He stared at the mountains.

"Really?" I cleared my throat. "Well, we were friends, and he started coming by and fixing things. He was very helpful."

"Uh-huh." Tony turned to study me coolly.

"He got mad when I tried to put some distance between us. He accused me of using him and shoved me."

"Don't worry. I'm not like that." He swatted a gnat away from his face. Bees buzzed among the wildflowers, and a sparrow hopped by on the sand, searching for bits of seed left by the chickens. A familiar silence grew.

I sighed and placed my hands in my lap. It felt enjoyable being next to Tony in the quiet late afternoon.

"I thought I'd never get out of that place," he murmured.

Feeling at a loss, I held my peace. The wind picked up and stirred the grass in the open fields. We simply sat next to each other, listening to the sounds of the countryside.

80·CB

Stanley spotted me a week later as I left the emporium. He streaked across the road, anxious to talk.

"Nina, wait up!"

I paused in front of my car. "Hi, Stanley."

He squinted happily, in better spirits than I could recall him in years. "Say, Nina, have you and Tony become friends again?"

I nodded. "Yes. Why do you ask?"

He shrugged. "Well, we all went out to dinner the other night, and a neighbor stopped by our table to say hello. Tony really went off on him."

It occurred to me that it had to have been Casey. "Gee, I'm sorry, Stanley. I probably shouldn't have said anything to Tony about it."

He waved me away. "Don't be sorry. It just surprised us to see Tony so annoyed. He's been distant and detached from everything since he came home. We've been worried about him. This was the first time Bess and I have actually seen him show a little life." He beamed and slapped my shoulder. "Thanks!"

ᘛ·ᘚ

"Casey came over for dinner the other night and told us you're dating Tony Kolinski!" Susanna exclaimed, her expression horrified as I entered our parents' living room for dinner the following Sunday afternoon.

I immediately felt on the defensive. "We're not dating."

"Casey said Tony threatened him in a restaurant over you!"

"If I were Casey, I wouldn't mess with someone just out of the slammer," Andrea commented, looking up from her crossword puzzle.

Our mother appeared shocked as well. "Did I hear you right?" she asked Susanna. "Did you say she's dating that Tony Kolinski?"

"We're just friends," I insisted. Truthfully, my schoolgirl crush had returned with a vengeance, but I was not about to admit it to any of them. "Anyway, so what if I were?"

"Because he's a drug addict, for one thing!" Susanna shot back, visibly angry. She'd arrived in a bad mood today and was finally able to vent her spleen.

My oldest brother, Matthew, squinted over at us, chewing on a cigar he wasn't allowed to light in the house. He and I were the only siblings who remained unmarried.

"Aw, he's not a bad guy. And he's paid his debt to society, right?"

"Don't marry him," my brother Jimmy pleaded. "He'll take you to the cleaners, just like he did his old man!" Jimmy was an investment fanatic.

Matthew waved Jimmy away. "Don't listen to him, Nina. I hear he's waiting tables at his father's restaurant every night after working on that farm all day. His father wants him to take over the place, and it's worth a fortune."

Susanna ignored Matthew and sighed, ready to give up on me yet another time.

"Well, I give up," she said, right on cue. "Casey is crazy about you, and he really needs help with those kids. If you want to mother something, why not marry him and actually make yourself useful?"

℥·Ω

It was sunset on a late Indian summer's day as I headed out of Farmdale Feed and Grain. The hills stretched out to the horizon, an expanse of endless gold in the lovely autumn evening. Peace enveloped me and time seemed to stand still, as if this moment were suspended beyond any other. Suddenly the world felt glorious, like everything had fallen perfectly into place.

A vehicle honked from behind and a blue Chevy truck pulled up and idled next to where I stood by the side of the road.

"Hey, Nina. Like my new truck?"

I studied Tony in surprise as he sat behind the wheel and nodded.

"I love it. It's perfect."

"Great," he replied as he reached over and opened the passenger door for me. "Because I bought it with you in mind."

A Touch of Evil

"This is really going to be a blast," Torrance pronounced as he gathered up his books and slipped into his navy blue jacket. "Just wait until the students find out that you're my uncle!"

Damon smiled and adjusted his glasses on his thin, ashen face as he gathered up the demonstration materials. A tuft of bushy, prematurely graying hair fell across his forehead, and he brushed it away.

"Let's hope I don't bore them to death."

"Oh, c'mon, you *couldn't*!" Torrance smoothed his conservatively styled brown hair to one side and pushed up his own glasses. "And thanks so much for agreeing to speak to my class. My teacher about flipped when she found out you're my uncle and that you'd be happy to give a talk."

Damon glanced over at his nephew. Torrance was afflicted with a disposition similar to his own—exceptional academic brilliance, yet utterly inept socially. This latest attempt to impress his peers was unlikely to succeed, but Damon suspected a young lady named Lilianna was the real motivation behind the lecture today. Torrance had taken a liking to the girl—a first, as far as Damon could recall, and it pained him to imagine his nephew undergoing the difficult passage into adulthood where romantic feelings play such an important part.

"Is Lilianna in your science class?" he asked in a way he hoped seemed offhand, leaning heavily on his cane as they walked out to his car parked in the drive. His leg ached today. A breeze stirred the hydrangeas, which were about to burst into bloom. The school year was three-quarters over.

Torrance squinted at him in surprise, not sure if he liked his uncle reading the heart that was pinned so obviously to his sleeve. Theirs had always been a world of complicated math calculations and intriguing science experiments. It seemed almost foreign to extend out from that comfortable realm. Torrance's unrequited romantic attachment weighed heavily on his mind, and the last thing he felt like doing was talking about it—to anyone.

"Yes," he finally replied as he clipped on his seatbelt.

Damon eased behind the wheel with difficulty and closed his eyes to recover from the sharp pain in his calf. A moment later, he stowed his cane across the back seat. His sister, Nancy, had informed him some time ago of Torrance's crush. For reasons he could no longer remember, she did not approve of the girl.

"I shall do my utmost to impress her." His smile softened the severity of his usual expression.

"Did Mom tell you she's a bad student?" Torrance asked. He studied his uncle for a moment. "Because she's not. She's actually quite gifted."

This was spoken from a true case of infatuation, Damon surmised, noting how Torrance was even unable to speak Lilianna's name. Suddenly, he recalled his sister's objection. Nancy had been concerned that the young lady would adversely affect Torrance's grades. But the school year was wrapping up, and Torrance, stricken with an incurable case of bashfulness, had been unable to express his feelings. Hence, he had maintained perfect marks, earning himself a full scholarship to the local university.

"It's just that she hangs around with that goofy Gabriel all the time. He likes to skip school and is a bad influence on her."

Damon remained silent and stared straight ahead as they sped in the direction of his nephew's school, hoping the morning would turn out well. He was, of course, unaware that the hour ahead would alter the course of his existence forever.

Twenty minutes later, Damon was greeted cordially by Mrs. Donovan. "Dr. Devereaux, it is *such* an honor to meet you!"

She smiled and clasped his hand. He returned the smile as his eyes swept the classroom. The students slouched in their seats, their eyes fixed stolidly ahead. Torrance had complained that he often felt persecuted for his genius by this particular class.

"Students, this is Dr. Damon Devereaux, one of the founders of the Woods Hollow Institute of Mathematical Physics. He's also engaged as a tenured professor at the university." She nodded at Torrance as he seated himself behind his desk across the room. "And he just so happens to be Torrance's uncle!"

A few of the students twisted in their chairs after a routine glance up at the clock.

"Do we have to take notes?" Little Chuckie, who was actually quite large, fished in a deplorable-looking notebook for a piece of paper that he hadn't already doodled on. His pencil fell out onto the mud-tracked floor. He scooped it up and clamped it securely between his teeth.

"Is any of this going to be on the test?" a heavily made-up girl called out without raising her hand. She winked at Damon and he looked away, regretting his decision years earlier not to finance his nephew's education at a private academy. He'd thought at the time that it would spoil Torrance and mire him in money and all it could provide, minus ethics and personal resolve. Nancy had never completely forgiven him, despite Torrance's excellent academic progress and recent scholarship.

Contemplating whether or not the scantily clad young woman might be Lilianna, Damon opened his briefcase for his notes while Mrs. Donovan attempted to subdue the class.

As the lecture began, a girl with shoulder-length brown hair, clutching a backpack, slipped into the room. Mrs. Donovan arose indignantly, as if this disruption were the last straw.

"Excuse me, Dr. Devereaux," she interrupted before turning back to the offending student. "Lilianna, you're fifteen minutes late. Your tardiness has interrupted our eminent guest, and as usual, created a distraction for the entire class. You are to spend the remainder of this period in study hall, and report for detention—"

"No, wait." Damon cast a quick glance at his nephew's crestfallen face before motioning to Lilianna. "Mrs. Donovan, my presentation requires an assistant. Let's have Lilianna help us out—a more suitable penalty, I'm sure." He smiled, and Lilianna, after noting her teacher's silence, weaved her way to the front of the class.

After a quick glimpse at her, Damon busied himself with some of the demonstration materials. Her round girlish face displayed a serious expression, yet her eyes were sweetly expressive when they met his. For some inexplicable reason, her presence rattled him.

A rush of lucidity overtook Damon and he realized how collapsed his spirit was. For an instant, he was privy to the full extent of the systemic abuse he'd tolerated during the ten years of his marriage, leading to his subsequent unrecognizable state of humanity. The deep shock of the revelation overwhelmed him, and the room began to blur. He felt the beginning of one of his spells. Born with a mild case of cerebral palsy, he'd been free of them for years, and had hoped they'd vanished for good.

Fighting against it, he faced the whiteboard and held on, aware of Lilianna as she leaned close in concern. He continued to weaken and feared that if he gripped the beveled ledge any tighter, it would snap.

He released it, about to go down. Lilianna grabbed him from behind and helped guide him to the floor while the class looked on in stunned silence. He simply lay there, struggling to breathe, while the room spun around before his eyes.

ඊ·ଔ

Two weeks after the science class fiasco, Damon moved into his recently purchased Victorian outside of town. Torrance borrowed his mother's car to stop by for a visit. After a quick tour, they sat outside on the back porch under the blossoming cherry tree.

"I'm so sorry I passed out on you like that," Damon began for the umpteenth time. "Really, I am."

"Don't worry about it," Torrance assured him. "It's just so boss the way you've agreed to host my study group in this awesome old house every week." Torrance pushed his glasses up and smoothed his hair into a perfect side part. "Mom is such a hoverer. It's embarrassing."

"Did you tell Nancy about the location switch?" Damon asked. He was certain she would not be pleased. His health had a tendency to worsen in the evening. Last night he had nearly fallen, but his fondness for Torrance overrode any misgivings.

"Not yet," Torrance admitted. As much as he loved his mother, he mourned the fact that he didn't have a father in the picture. The appearance of Uncle Damon in his life had quickly closed the gap.

"Would you like me to explain it to her?"

"That would be boss!"

Damon smiled, amused by his nephew's slang. "Consider it done."

ಬ·ಅ

"Whatever possessed you to buy that old house, Damon? All three stories need renovation." Nancy shook her head in distress. After his relocation to Woods Hollow, she'd expected him to buy a nice condo near the university.

"It's an investment." Damon hid behind the morning paper.

Nancy remained doubtful. The majority of her brother's investments were conservative and easy to manage. The purchase of the Victorian on the outskirts of town seemed completely out of character. The angular cross-gabled structure, half-hidden in a grove of mulberry trees, presented like an isolated specter as one passed by on the road. She didn't like the idea of his living there at all.

"So you don't plan to live there permanently?" She placed her hands on his shoulders.

"I didn't say that."

She appeared dumbfounded. "But that place is a shambles."

He patted her hand. "It's not as bad as that. And I've hired a renovator. He'll be living in the cottage at the end of the drive. He's making the main floor livable as we speak."

It annoyed Nancy that Damon had never breathed a word to her about this until now. She'd heard of Donte being engaged as the caretaker from her friend, Jane.

"That man has a criminal record."

Damon's eyes appeared over the top of the page. "It was a minor drug infraction. Really, Nancy, it happened years ago, and he was a teenager at the time."

"Will he pay anything to live at the cottage?" The cottage was in good condition and could secure a tidy rent, as far as she knew.

"No."

Nancy gazed out the window to where Torrance and his friend Jase stood conversing on the drive. Renovating a structure that would be better pulled down and hiring a freeloader to do it seemed like a money drain to her. The funds could have been invested in Torrance's education instead.

"Torrance has applied to MIT."

"I think he should attend the university here," Damon insisted for the umpteenth time. "He has a full scholarship already."

"Well, he doesn't agree, and neither do I," Nancy responded, careful not to lose her temper.

Damon folded the paper and stood up. "Let's just see if he's accepted." Torrance would only be seventeen when he started his freshman year. "Education isn't everything, Nancy."

"How can you say that?" she exclaimed. "You received the best education money could buy and ended up one of the most intelligent men in the world!"

A shadow fell across her brother's face. "I'd like to spare him a similar fate."

"You had no control over what happened to you. And don't worry, I plan to watch out for him. I'm just glad Lilianna Annesley spends most of her time with Gabriel Cordova."

According to Damon's physician friend, Dr. Henry Sorenson, Gabriel was afflicted with Thalassemia Major and very ill, but he felt disinclined to discuss it with his sister. Henry had mentioned to him how overly protective Gabriel's parents were regarding their only child's fragile health.

"Lilianna seems like a very charming young lady."

"That's what you think," Nancy countered. "I heard that Naomi asked Lilianna to stop monopolizing Gabriel's time. She even went so far as to call the girl's father to complain about it."

Damon wondered if Naomi frowned upon the friendship because it caused her son to exert himself too much. "She may not realize how ill he is."

"Sure, she does," Nancy replied. "Last year, Mrs. Crabtree published a poem in the school paper that Lilianna wrote about Gabriel's illness without her permission. Lilianna had some kind of outburst right in front of the class, refused to complete the rest of her assignments, and received a D in English instead. She told Mrs. Crabtree she'd violated her privacy and that she'd never write another poem again as long as she lived."

Nancy studied Damon with amusement.

"Torrance asked me to host his study group twice a week."

"You don't have to do that. They can study right here like they always have. Really, Dames, you don't need to—"

"I don't mind." Torrance had pleaded with him. His nephew desperately hoped Lilianna would join the group if it were no longer held at his house.

"But you're not feeling well with that low grade infection going. You need to rest in the evenings. I know how tired you get."

"Henry said I'm improving."

Nancy doubted it. Under that mop of unruly hair and pronounced mustache, her brother's face often appeared strained with fatigue.

"I appreciate all you do for Torrance. But don't do anything if you don't feel up to it."

⚭·⚬

"What do we have going for snacks?" Torrance asked as he peered into the pantry. Lilianna had just returned from a trip to see her sister and would most likely be at the study group tonight, despite Gabriel no longer being permitted to attend. She seemed to be enjoying the gathering without Gabby's attendance and had yet to miss a session. In fact, Lilianna often arrived before the rest of the group.

Damon smiled. "Everything your friends like, including Lilianna."

"Great." He rubbed his hands together. Damon fell silent. He was looking forward to spending a moment with Lilianna himself, but it troubled him to see Torrance so enamored with a girl who did not return his feelings. She liked Gabriel, but Torrance refused to give up hope.

"What's the matter?" Torrance asked.

"Nothing. Just considering the idiosyncrasies of life."

"Mom thinks you're behaving intractably over Jane. She's convinced she's the perfect woman for you." Torrance laughed. "I shouldn't tell you this, but she's planning on inviting her over for dinner the next time you come. She's scheming to have Jane 'accidentally' drop by."

"Really?" Damon grew irritated, but concealed it from Torrance.

"Uh-huh. She's sure you'll be crazy about her once you get to know her."

"I do know her. We've worked on projects together."

"Do you like her?"

"I wish your mother would stop acting like I'm a teenager. I'm an old man."

Torrance smiled. "You're not that old. You're still young."

"I'm too old for her plots."

Torrance sighed. "I sure wish she liked Lilianna. You like Lilianna, don't you?" He studied his uncle with hope.

"Yes." Damon nodded, sadness filling him. "She's a lovely person."

Torrance beamed. "That makes me feel so much better."

Damon wanted to warn Torrance about the perils of unrequited love, but his own disarrayed life prevented it. But one thing was certain—he wouldn't be accepting any dinner invitations from his sister in the future.

ℬ·ℭ

"So you're turning eighteen next week," Damon remarked as he replaced the book Lilianna had handed him on the bookshelf. Torrance had lent it to her earlier in the week with the explanation that it belonged to his uncle's private collection at the university.

Lilianna beamed, pleased to have discovered Damon alone. She'd spotted Torrance at the library not long ago and hastened to Damon's office. Fortunately, she'd also avoided Nancy.

"I'm going to be nineteen," she corrected. "I was held back in the third grade because I had meningitis and missed a lot of school."

"And what do you want for your nineteenth birthday?" Damon asked. He turned to study her with a smile.

She shrugged. "Oh, nothing, I guess."

"Nothing?" He laughed. "You can say that when you're ninety, but not at nineteen, for heaven's sake."

"My grandmother just turned ninety. She wanted a crock pot."

"Well, I hope you don't want a crock pot."

"No." It was her turn to laugh.

"What if the sky were the limit?"

She grew silent.

"What about working with children?" Torrance had told him how devoted she was to children.

"I'd like that."

"Would you like to become a teacher?"

She scrunched up her amiable face. "Not really."

"How about social work?"

"No, I don't think so. I'd really like to get married and have my own children."

The admission surprised him. Obviously she didn't realize the gravity of Gabriel's affliction.

"Perhaps that might be a better idea when you're a little older."

"My grandmother married when she was seventeen. My grandparents were married for sixty-nine years."

"Gabriel is very ill."

"I didn't mean marry Gabriel. I know how sick he is."

He regarded her thoughtfully. Did she have feelings for Torrance after all?

"It's a good idea to get an education first. For example, Torrance plans to—"

"I didn't mean marry your nephew either."

"I wasn't assuming that," he replied quickly. "I was merely conjecturing." Despite their comfortable friendship, he realized there were aspects to Lilianna he'd failed to grasp.

"I'd like to marry you, though."

The blood drained from his face. He felt as though he might faint.

"Are you all right?" she asked.

He laughed to conceal his own distress. "I'm fine." The blood returned to his head. He had narrowly escaped passing out.

"I didn't mean it literally," she explained. "I just meant it as a compliment. I'm really sorry if it upset you."

"I'm all right." He forced a smile.

"Well, I feel awful."

"I'm flattered, Lilianna. Really, I am. But I'd be a terrible catch and I'm too old for you."

"I shouldn't have said anything."

He patted her arm. "There's no harm done."

She nodded. "All right. I need to be going."

He showed her to the door, still feeling uncomfortable. "Goodbye, Lilianna."

She started down the path for the woods, but turned for a final look.

"And you're not that old, you know!" she called out to him.

Damon sighed and slipped back into his office.

ɞ·ʗଷ

That evening, Damon held a mirror to the back of his leg. The skin was warm to the touch and necrotic tissue was plainly evident. He decided to call the clinic and schedule another debriding of the ulcerated bite. Staring at the misshapen calf and lumpy reddened tissue, he recalled his consultation with the specialist not long ago. If the bite continued to ulcerate, there would be no other option except to amputate.

He placed the mirror on his nightstand and considered the harebrained miscalculation he'd made earlier in the month that had significantly derailed the Institute's latest research project. Humiliation filled him. His colleagues had not handled the gaffe charitably. The Institute no longer seemed an affable place; he'd been deluding himself in the past—much like his ten-year marriage.

He glanced across the room at the windows lining the wall. It was a damp night and a mist had formed over the glass. The reflection of the trees struck an arresting pattern on the panes. He studied the effect in silence. The loveliness of it moved him, and for a moment, he experienced a fragile glimmer of hope.

Awakening during the night to a sharp stab of pain in his leg, he thought fleetingly of Lilianna. The truth was suddenly palpable as he lay all alone in the darkness. If he were younger and without the emotional and physical scars he carried, he would have fallen deeply in love with Lilianna.

ɞ·ʗଷ

"Things are looking reasonably well," Dr. Henry Sorenson

assured Damon during the medical check following the debridement procedure. "Your leg looks about the same as before. That's a plus. The lesion is no longer in an exorable state of deterioration. How have you been feeling?"

"At times I have trouble walking, but otherwise, I can't complain." Damon slipped his undershirt over his thin frame.

"We'll have to get Nancy to fatten you up," Henry joked. "Have you considered moving back in with her and Torrance? She told me she'd love to have you. And you're a great influence on your nephew... exactly what he needs right now."

Damon shook his head. "I don't think that would be a good idea."

Henry replaced the stethoscope on its hook. "Why not?"

"It's safer if I live alone."

"I doubt she'll ever try anything again. Granted, it was impossible to prove she planted the spiders in your bed, but she's an entomologist and remains permanently under suspicion. She'd be a fool to risk it, and she's anything but that." He glanced away, wishing for his friend's sake that the woman in question were dead. She'd been his patient in year's past and nearly succumbed to cancer. But life had granted her a reprieve, and she had chosen to poison her husband with it.

It was obvious that even now, after so much time had elapsed, Damon was not able to put it behind him either psychologically or physically. His body remained weakened and fragile from the nearly lethal bites, and his leg was chronically ulcerated, despite every effort to treat it.

"I refuse to involve them in my problems. It could be dangerous."

Henry shook his head. "By problems, do you mean your decision to get married?"

"Yes, and everything that occurred in the years since. It's bad enough I returned to Woods Hollow. She still has a million dollar life insurance policy on me."

Henry shrugged. "I think she realizes that it would be impossible to escape scrutiny if anything suspicious happened to you. And don't forget, we *all* liked her. Everyone thought she was a wonderful person. None of us is immune to being deceived."

Damon finished dressing in silence.

"Gabriel Cordova passed away last night," Henry remarked, his expression grave.

Damon looked up. "My God, that's tragic."

"Yes, it was quite sudden, although not unexpected. His heart just gave out."

Damon sighed, the news a shock nevertheless. Torrance was away at Bear Mountain, arranging the senior class trip. His thoughts drifted to Lilianna.

"How tragic," he repeated, as he buttoned his shirt.

"The funeral is planned for later in the week, if you can make it."

Damon smoothed his hair and slipped on his glasses. "Of course I'll make it. We'll all be there."

⅜·⅝

"Torrance—" Damon drew a deep breath and attempted to collect himself. "You can't miss the funeral. It wouldn't be right." He wondered how his nephew could abandon Lilianna at such a heart-rending hour. "There will be plenty of trips in your life, I assure you."

Torrance shook his head. "Not like this one." He studied his uncle a moment. "It took months of planning to set it up. It's unfortunate Gabriel passed away right now, but I can't just abandon my class after they put all their faith in me regarding this trip. That wouldn't be right. Don't you see?"

Damon frowned. "Franky, I don't. The itinerary is set. Whether you're there or not shouldn't impact the trip in any significant way. Besides, you can go up after the funeral and catch the remainder of things. But if you miss—"

"I'm not ditching my friends and that's all there is to it!" Torrance grabbed his trigonometry folder and prepared to clear out.

"What about Lilianna? How about being there for her?"

Torrance paused for a moment at the kitchen door. "Gabriel's dead. I'm as sorry about it as anyone else, and I feel for Lilianna. But I have to go on this trip. I can offer support to Lilianna later. Got it?"

His imperious tone stung. Damon was forced to acknowledge that a change had occurred in their relationship. Torrance had been accepted into MIT, and because of Damon's reluctance to support the decision, the bond of trust between them had begun to erode.

He held his peace. Torrance slammed the door behind him. Damon grabbed the phone to call his sister.

"Hello?"

"Hi, Nancy. Torrance just left for school. He says he's not going to miss the trip to go to the funeral. I tried to talk to him, but got nowhere."

There was no response on her part.

"Nancy? Are you there?"

"Yes."

"Did you hear what I said?"

"Dames, it's his decision."

"How can you say that? He's known that boy since elementary school."

"I know, but this trip means a great deal to him."

Suddenly Damon trembled. He'd left the window open and it was a stormy morning. Was he coming down with something?

"All right, Nancy."

"I wish you wouldn't let this upset you."

"There's nothing more to be said." Damon could not shake the ill feeling. Like his situation at the Institute, the solidity of his relationships with Nancy and Torrance was coming under fire, and he was edging toward a depressing realignment of his thinking. "Goodbye, Nancy."

℥·℣

"I'm telling you, it's true. You just can't see it," Jase insisted, his long legs propped on the fence rail as he sat perched in the cherry tree outside Damon's back door. "She's sweet on your uncle."

"No way." Torrance laughed. "She's just been down over Gabby, and he's trying to cheer her up. My uncle's practically an old man."

"He is to you because he's your uncle. And she's nineteen, don't forget."

Nancy approached from the drive where she'd left her car idling. "Hey, you two. Ready to go?"

Torrance waved. "Hi, Mom."

"We'd better run if you want me to take you by the theater," Nancy said as she looked around for her brother. "I'm going to Jane's house after I drop you off, remember? Is Dames around?"

Torrance shook his head. "No, he took Lilianna and her sister Emily to the cemetery. Donte gave them a rose bush for Gabriel's grave."

"They have rose bushes on sale at the emporium," Nancy remarked while scanning the house. The place appeared noticeably improved.

"I'd already offered them one from the property," a voice broke in. They all turned to discover Donte standing next to the cherry tree.

"That was nice of you," Nancy responded, though her expression appeared displeased.

"That rose bush technically belonged to my uncle," Torrance informed him. He'd developed an aversion to the taciturn Donte and the Victorian house in general. Now graduated and no longer holding his study sessions here, he found it difficult to understand his uncle's rationale for living so far out of town. The house was costing far more to renovate than Damon had originally expected. And Torrance would never be able to stay at the guest cottage on breaks from school either, like he'd hoped. Donte planned to continue his services as a groundskeeper after the completion of the renovation work.

Donte shrugged and adjusted his sweatband. "I needed to remove it anyway to extend the woodshed."

"Lovely," Nancy replied, refusing to look him in the eye. "We have to be going."

"Later, Donte," Jase managed as he hurried to catch up with Nancy and Torrance. "And it was nice of you to give Gabby the rose bush—"

℘·℘

A week later, Damon rounded the curve in his drive to discover Donte waiting for him. The handyman wore a pensive look.

"Everything okay?" Damon asked as he opened his mail box and sorted through the letters.

"They're waiting for you inside. I told them you were out for a walk."

"All right." Damon knew from Donte's expression that he meant Torrance and Nancy. "Wish they'd call first."

"They don't look happy."

"Thanks for the warning." Damon turned for the front porch. Torrance had left several messages earlier asking for additional funds for his college expenses. Damon assumed they were upset because he had yet to get back to them.

"What's up?" Damon tossed his mail aside as he entered the house and studied the two of them guardedly. Nancy and Torrance were seated next to each other on the sofa.

"It's this!" Torrance held out a piece of paper accusingly. His expression appeared incensed. He stood up and walked over.

Damon snatched the paper and scanned it with a frown. It was an introspective, skillfully composed piece of poetry extolling the virtues of true love.

"I'm afraid I don't understand."

Torrance glared. "It's a poem."

"I can see that. But what does it have to do with me?"

"Turn it over and look at the other side. It was written for you... by Lilianna!"

Damon's eyes widened in surprise. "Where did you get it?"

"A girl from school found it in a book Lilianna had returned to the library. Now all my friends know about it, and I get why she wanted to be in the study group even though Gabby couldn't come!"

"This is a terrible violation of her privacy."

"She's obviously set her sights on your money, Dames," Nancy said, breaking her silence. "It would be a mistake to think otherwise."

Damon folded the piece of paper and slipped it into his shirt pocket.

"I want that back," Torrance insisted.

"Well, you're not getting it."

"What are you going to do with it?" Nancy asked, her expression aggrieved.

"I plan to return it."

"Do I need to remind you that she just graduated high school?" his sister chided. "I'm sure it's flattering, but you're too old for her."

"Why do you think I'd be flattered when you assume she's after my money?"

"What went on at that funeral?" Torrance asked, wondering if they'd missed some clue along the way.

Damon grew stoical. Torrance had gone to Bear Mountain and Nancy had dined with friends.

"I heard from Jane that you sat with her," Nancy said.

"I want you both to leave."

"You should have just left her alone!" Torrance declared, his eyes flashing. "Why didn't you sit with someone your own age, like Jane?"

"You shouldn't have gone to Bear Mountain, but that was the choice you made."

"Well, you shouldn't have gone to the funeral at all!" Torrance shot back. "I want you to stay away from my friends!"

"Leave!" Damon was a hair's breadth from losing his temper.

Nancy reached for her purse and cast her brother a doubtful look. "I hope you're telling us the truth. You don't need another gold digger in your life. You still haven't recovered from the last one."

Damon held the door open for them. "Just go!"

"We care about you," were her final words. "We truly do."

Damon slammed the door behind them and collapsed in a chair. He covered his eyes. A moment later, he glanced out the window. The canopy of mulberry trees waved in the afternoon light and cast a captivating shadow across the far wall. The moving branches calmed him. A robin flew by the window and landed nearby, its melodious song filling the air.

He pulled the poem from his pocket and slowly reread the contents. She had sworn never to write another, and yet she had... for him. It pleased him immensely to consider that fact. Unfortunately, he couldn't keep it.

ಐ·ೞ

Henry watched from the third floor window of his office as

his friend maneuvered himself slowly into his car in the parking lot below. Something in his patient's manner of movement upset the physician, yet he could not identify the reason for his apprehension. He had just delivered good news to Damon, yet his patient's reaction seemed less enthusiastic than expected. Damon's leg was the cause of his difficulty walking, but Henry sensed an oppression around his friend as he watched him struggle to slip behind the wheel of his car.

Perhaps it could be attributed to the recent complications at the Institute, which Damon had admitted to be beset with infighting and professional jealousies. Or possibly it might be the funding cuts at the university that had derailed his research. With a distraught shake of his head, Henry sensed it traveled deeper than that. It seemed to him that, despite the support of friends and family and a successful career, the dark events of the past had severed a connection in Damon to some force critical to his recovery. The leg could be salvaged. Henry was not so sure about the outcome of the sear on his friend's soul.

ଚଠ · ଓଓ

Donte pulled his truck up alongside Damon's Impala where it was parked in the lot beside the Institute. He rolled down his window and leaned out.

"Are you headed home?"

Damon nodded and turned the key in the ignition. "Yes, I'm calling it a day."

"Well, I'm driving out to see my mom and brother for the evening."

"Have a nice visit."

"Nancy and Torrance are up at the house."

"Torrance is back?"

"Yes. He returned from Cambridge this afternoon."

Damon frowned. "Thanks for the heads-up."

With a brusque smile, Donte adjusted his sunglasses and pulled away.

At home, Damon discovered his sister and nephew seated on the sofa again, but this time their expressions seemed animated and hopeful.

"What's up?" Damon asked.

"Did you talk to Henry?" Nancy asked.

"Yes." His expression remained dour.

"Well, what do you think? He told us about the ground-breaking new treatment available at the clinic in New York. They remove all your blood and run it through a machine before—"

"I already know—he told me."

"You have to give it a try!" Torrance exclaimed as he jumped up from the couch.

"Yes," Nancy insisted. "There's a very good possibility that you might actually get well."

"We're super excited about it," Torrance continued. "But at the same time... cautiously optimistic."

Damon's expression remained unreadable.

Nancy stood up and reached for his shoulder. "Really, Dames, you don't know how much this news of Henry's means to us."

"Just think of it," Torrance said. "You could be well."

Damon pulled away from his sister and turned around to face them. "Well?" he said at last. "And what in God's name makes you think I want to be well?"

❧ · ☙

Henry gazed up at the house, his expression amazed. "This has turned out to be a beautiful place. How many windows on the second floor?"

"Seven," Damon replied. "And eight on the first."

"They're large enough, too. You could easily fit five children into a place this size." Henry treasured his large family, several of whom were adopted.

Damon laughed. "That's hardly likely."

Henry studied his friend. "Why not? You could certainly afford it."

"I'm sure this is not the reason you drove all the way out here," Damon stated.

"Actually, I'm on my way out of town, but I wanted to stop by and tell you in person that your initial procedure is scheduled for the first Tuesday of next month."

Damon grew quiet. He examined a rose bloom on a bush Donte had transplanted near the porch.

"Is that all right?"

Damon nodded. "Yes."

"Good." Henry regarded Damon equably. "I have a good feeling about this, Damon."

"Okay, Henry. I trust you implicitly."

Henry laughed. "Now *that* worries me."

೮೦·೮ಚ

"Lilianna!" Damon stood and waved his newspaper above the crowd gathered at the University Bistro.

She turned and spotted him. With a smile, she came over.

"It's so nice to see you!" she exclaimed as he rose to pull out a chair.

"How have you been?" he asked. The autumn leaves circled down from the maple trees in the afternoon breeze and brushed against their table.

"I'm fine, thank you." Lilianna felt a twinge of discomfiture despite her delight over seeing him again. Even with a year's passage, the embarrassment over the ill-fated love sonnet was proving hard to live down.

"I'm glad to hear it," Damon replied. "Henry told me you're employed at the girls' academy."

"Yes, that's right," she acknowledged as a server poured her a cup of coffee. "This week I was the laundress." She smiled. "And next week I'll be the cook."

"You have a school full of children, then."

"Yes." She looked away. The remark jogged another painful memory best left forgotten. "Is Torrance back in Cambridge?" she asked, anxious to change the topic.

"Yes, he's started his sophomore year." Damon sipped his coffee. "He has a girlfriend now. Her name is Bristol."

"That's nice." She breathed a surreptitious sigh of relief.

"You and I have been out of touch for a long while," he began. "Actually, I've been away receiving treatment for a medical condition. I only returned recently."

Lilianna nodded. "I hope it turned out all right. Where did you go?"

"New York. And it was entirely successful."

"I'm so happy to hear it." It occurred to her how well he seemed compared to a year ago. He no longer appeared gaunt, and his complexion had lost its ashen pallor. "You look wonderful," she said before she could stop herself.

"Thank you. You're too kind."

Lilianna stirred her coffee to conceal her emotions. "Actually, I'm too candid."

It was an enchanting afternoon, with great cumulus clouds visible through the openings between the picturesque old trees adjoining the courtyard.

"I'll have to disagree," he replied, his expression thoughtful. "And I'm so glad we ran into each other."

She set her cup down. "I'm enrolled in several poetry classes this semester."

"That's wonderful."

"I'm writing a book of verse for children," Lilianna continued, laughing. "I hope to stay out of trouble that way."

"I thought the poem you wrote for me was rather extraordinary."

"*You're* too kind."

They smiled as another cascade of leaves drifted down, scattering in every direction.

⅋·⅌

"Are you sure you won't have dinner with us?" Nancy asked, having stopped by the Victorian.

"I already have a dinner date," Damon replied as he straightened his tie while studying his reflection in the mirror.

Torrance stepped into the room. "Are you two coming? Bristol is anxious to leave. I made the reservations for seven."

Nancy shook her head. "Damon already has plans."

"Can you possibly get out of them? Bristol and I are only here for the weekend."

"I'm not cancelling."

Nancy brightened. "Are you having dinner with Jane, by chance? Why not join us at Del La Rosa's?"

"My date is not with Jane."

"Is it business?" Nancy asked, noting how smartly he was dressed.

"No." Damon reached for his jacket.

"Why the reticence?" Torrance asked, impatient to join Bristol downstairs. "Why not tell us with whom you prefer to dine instead of us?"

Damon turned to face them. "I saw Lilianna earlier today and asked her to have dinner with me."

"Lilianna?" Torrance repeated in disbelief.

"Dames," Nancy began, "you can't be serious."

"I'm afraid I am, and I'll have to say goodnight."

Nancy trailed after him with Torrance at her heels. "I thought this was all water under the bridge. Why dredge it back up?"

His expression grew resolute. "Because I've given this a great deal of thought, and you know what?"

"What?" they asked in unison.

He smiled. "I'm really not that old."

Hardship House

It should have been a picture-perfect day, the morning Katie and Danny moved into Hardship House—as she would later call it. Two months previously, the purchase of the Craftsman bungalow had been a dream come true. But move-in day greeted them with a miserable drizzle of rain that clung to Danny's recent medical diagnoses like a shroud.

"Don't overdo it," Katie cautioned her husband, instantly regretting the words.

Danny's long, handsome face froze in an expression of sorrow. "I'll take it easy," he promised, his tall form framed by the doorway as he paused with a box.

Katie looked away to conceal her own sadness. He appeared so attractive and sound, but his weakening and becoming disabled before his thirty-third birthday was more likely than not, according to the doctors. After the troubling news, they'd debated whether or not to move into the house at all. It was uncertain how long he would continue to work, and they'd have to put off, perhaps indefinitely, having children to fill the household they'd imagined together. But it seemed easier to proceed as planned and take their new, ambiguous existence together one day at a time.

Danny placed the box on a table and turned for the paned double doors that led out to the garden. "I'm going to have a look out back," he called to Katie where she stood with the movers at the front door.

She smiled. "Sounds good!" she sang out a bit too cheerfully.

Out in the misting garden, he glanced around in dismay. The shrubs had exploded over the summer with riotous growth in every direction. The lengthy terraced yard had initially charmed Danny, but as he looked around, his enthusiasm changed to trepidation. He leaned against a makeshift table. It collapsed under his weight and shattered on the uneven brick walkway. It seemed to him a bad omen.

"Everything all right?" Katie shouted, still wearing the smile. The movers waited patiently behind her.

Danny nodded and brushed off his trousers. "Just fine," he replied, his face a mask. "I had a little mishap."

Katie stared a moment at the pieces of wood before disappearing inside. Perhaps she felt it too. His eyes traveled up to the deep roof eaves. He shook his head, despondency filling him.

"Why did I have to get sick?" he murmured.

The towering big-leaf maples stirred in a sudden gust of wind. A wave of lethargy struck him and, closing his eyes, he dozed for a moment on his feet. He then jolted awake again and felt an electrical force pass through his nerve cells.

"*Everybody's sick,*" the trees seemed to sigh in reply through the patter of rain and fragrant breezes that wafted through the shrubbery.

"Danny?" Katie stood at the doors. "Come in out of the rain before you catch your—"

She caught herself.

He turned in her direction, the rain obscuring his silhouette. With a final defeated look at the splintered boards, he started back for the house.

᛫ᛒᛒ᛫ᛍᛍ᛫

"Are you going to work after your doctor's appointment to-day?" Katie asked as she buttoned her white silk blouse. It was Monday morning and boxes were still strewn everywhere. Danny had felt exhausted all weekend, slowing down their progress.

"Yes, for a half day." Despite his ill health, he felt compelled to keep working to afford their sizable mortgage. Katie's employment as a legal assistant paid well, but she planned to return to law school in the fall for her final year. He wondered if his prognosis would spell the end of another dream of hers. Guilt tore away at him.

"Okay." She kissed his cheek. "See you later tonight."

"If Lyndsey would like to eat out this evening, you should go." Until recently, it had been their custom to dine with Katie's twin sister Monday evenings.

"Oh no," Katie assured him, turning her girlish face away and brushing her straight brown hair. "I don't want to go if you—"

"I insist." He gently touched her on the shoulder, a head taller than she as he smiled down at her. "I doubt I'll have much of an appetite. It'll be an opportunity for me to rest and for the two of you to catch up."

"All right." After a quick hug, she hurried downstairs and raced across the broad front porch and down the steps leading to the tree-lined street below. He was watching from the window when she turned to wave from between the tapered columns. He returned the gesture, but once she was out of sight, his smile vanished.

᛫ᛒᛒ᛫ᛍᛍ᛫

Katie drove away in her Fiat and turned the corner before pulling over to the curb. After ensuring no one was around, she folded her arms across the steering wheel and cried.

ஓ·ଓ

Later that evening in the dimly lit master bedroom, Danny unpacked several boxes of clothing and arranged his undershirts in the drawers of a dresser. His body felt heavy and every movement proved laborious. He had intended to work for an hour, but eyed the bed with longing. All he wanted to do was lie down and sleep forever.

He opened another box and winced upon the discovery of more clothing. His effervescent young wife was a clothes horse. With a pounding head, he arranged her skirts on clip hangers and hung them next to his dress shirts, recalling how only a short time ago he'd pulled fourteen-hour work days and still had energy to spare upon meeting Katie at home for a late night dinner.

Darkness was falling and the wind began to blow. Gusts whirled up under the eaves where they rattled the house. He glanced out the multi-paned window over the garden as the trees lashed back and forth in the gathering storm. A fluffy white cat appeared and scurried away through an opening in the fence. Rain pelted against the glass. Reaching over to pull the curtain closed, Danny wished Katie were home. He felt like a coward, but all alone in the old house with a potential death sentence hanging over his head propelled him back to his boyhood fear of the dark.

Just before he drew the curtains shut, he thought he spotted something below on the walkway. Parting them again, he frowned, attempting to peer through the rivulets of water running across the glass. It looked like a child running out in the rain.

"Danny, I'm home!" Katie called out from the front entryway.

He turned in the direction of her voice. "In here!" he shouted, and then turned back to the window again. The walkway was deserted.

"What are you looking at?" Katie asked when she stood beside him a minute later and slipped her arm around him.

"I saw a little girl on the footpath."

"In this weather?" Katie looked out the window. There was only the uneven movement of branches obscured by the falling rain. "Perhaps it was the wheelbarrow."

He turned away, his expression strained. She noticed dark circles under his eyes. It hit her hard, the drawn look on his face. It was the first moment she'd noticed the encroachment of disease in his physical appearance. It felt like a slice on her heart and she looked away, busying herself with her jewelry.

"It must have been my imagination playing tricks on me again," Danny mused. He thought of the whispering maples. "I always wanted a little girl."

"Really?" Katie asked.

"Yes. I wanted to name her Lily."

Katie hesitated as she unclasped the locket around her neck, a present from Danny on their first wedding anniversary. He spoke as though their life together was already finished, his death imminent, and any hope of children gone— like the specter in the storm.

"We shouldn't give up hope," she managed. "The doctors did say they weren't absolutely certain about your outcome."

Silence ensued, and long after the lights were out, they both lay awake in the darkness, listening to the pounding rain.

∓·∞

As the summer advanced to a close, Danny worked less and puttered around the house more. His progress with any renovation work proved slow, however, and he often found himself staring out the middle window of the front dormer instead. Once an avid reader, he found it now hurt his head

too much to concentrate. The world beyond the glass became more intriguing each day as he grew to recognize the
trees, birds, neighborhood cats and dogs, and the people
who passed by his line of vision.

One neighbor in particular captivated him—a gentleman
in his late sixties who walked with the assistance of a cane.
The man always appeared well-dressed, but he navigated
with a dreadful limp that greatly affected his movement. Day
after day, Danny watched as his neighbor skillfully stowed
his cane and slipped precariously into his vehicle, adept at
managing the challenging disability.

"What's so interesting?" Katie inquired one afternoon.
As she leaned in next to him, she spied their neighbor ma-
neuvering to his car.

"That man out there."

Katie watched as well. "Yes, he has a bit of grandeur
about him. I've noticed it before."

"He reminds me of you," Danny said.

Katie smiled to herself. "And why ever is that?"

"You have that same quality. I noticed it the first time I
saw you."

Lyndsey had introduced them at a gathering in her home
two years earlier. "I almost didn't go to my sister's that
night," she admitted, noting him shiver in the late afternoon
coolness that had crept into the house.

"That wasn't the first time."

"Really?" Katie asked, surprised.

"Yes."

"Wrap this around you," she instructed as she turned up
the furnace. She handed him his favorite blue blanket.

"I saw you at a Halloween party."

She shook her head. "I don't remember that."

"You were dressed as a macabre Mary Queen of Scots."

Katie started. "I was fourteen years old!"

"I know."

"You were there?" The party had been held at a church she'd attended as a child.

"Yes."

She drew a deep breath. Danny must have been twenty-two at the time. "Well, I can't imagine why you'd ever remember me."

"You were showing off your costume to all your mother's friends. You were so regal and self-possessed."

It occurred to Katie, not for the first time, how oddly endearing her husband was. She placed her arms around him and rested her head on his shoulder as they watched their neighbor drive away.

℘·℘

"Here, kitty, kitty, kitty!" Danny called out to the vacant garden. Only a moment earlier, he'd spotted a fluffy white cat disappear through the gap in the fence again. His eyes did a quick sweep of the groundcover, half expecting to see the little girl. Dry maple leaves scattered about in the breeze, and a passing flock of sparrows alighted nearby. He turned back for the kitchen door, but just before he closed it, he spotted a child running beyond the maples. He strode quickly to the edge of the lawn and peered around the corner.

The alley was deserted.

℘·℘

"We're back!" Katie called out. It was another Monday evening, and thanks to Lyndsey's assistance, the moving in had long since been completed.

Danny was reclining in a chair, completely wiped out from another round of antibiotics. He glanced up from his newspaper.

"How was dinner?" he asked his wife and sister-in-law.

"Great. We dined at the Star Marina," Katie replied.

"You should come along some time when you're feeling better," Lyndsey suggested with a smile. His appearance alarmed her, but she made every effort not to show any distress.

"I don't know if I'm going to be feeling better," he responded dryly, turning back to his paper. He knew his bleak attitude was wearing away at Katie, but lately he couldn't seem to amend it. The constant feeling of systemic wretchedness weakened his resolve to do better.

"I'm betting you will." Lyndsey patted the top of his head. "We'll take you out for a night on the town."

"Splendid." He rubbed his tired eyes, and both sisters noticed the rash that had spread up his arm.

"Did you show that to the doctor?" Katie asked.

"Yes. They gave me a big shot in the rear and it's going to go away."

"Sounds like a fun day," Lyndsey remarked as she handed him a small present.

"What's this?" Danny asked, attempting to conceal his pleasure. He loved being the recipient of gifts.

"A get-well present."

"Hope it's not edible," he mumbled as he tore off the wrapper. Inside was a St. Jude medal suspended on a glistening silver chain.

"It's perfect," he mumbled, coiling it back into the box again. "Absolutely appropriate." His sarcasm was palpable.

Lyndsey leaned down and kissed his cheek. "It's late. I'll let the two of you get some rest."

After seeing her sister to the door, Katie discovered her husband already in his pajamas, staring out the bedroom window at the garden below.

"It wasn't meant to imply that you're hopeless," Katie began, pulling the tie loose that held her hair. She increasingly felt under tremendous strain. With each passing day, the solid bond of intimacy between them seemed to be wearing thinner. "You're the brightest and the best."

The flickering light of the streetlamp through the trees illumed his haggard face. He did not appear pleased.

"How I've always hated that."

Katie frowned. "What?"

"That maxim… the brightest and the best. What does it make everyone else?" Danny fell silent, awaiting her reply.

"I didn't mean to upset you." She turned away and rolled her eyes.

"You didn't answer my question."

Katie experienced a twinge of anger. The relationship had grown one-sided. She sensed that no matter what she said, it would backfire on her. "Well, I suppose it would make them the stupidest and the worst," she ventured while she combed out her hair.

He studied her quietly for a moment. She hesitated and watched his reflection in the mirror. The dimly lit room concealed his ill appearance, and from where she was seated, he looked well again.

Suddenly, Danny laughed and, removing the medal from its container, he slipped it over his head. "Make sure you bury me in this."

„·’

Katie's father handed her a sizable check. "Take this. You'll need it to finish your degree. If Danny's situation doesn't improve, you may have to support him indefinitely." He pushed a shock of lanky silver hair back from his deep-set blue eyes and smiled with encouragement.

Katie put her arms around him in gratitude and rested her head against his shoulder. It felt wonderful to be comforted and taken care of for a change, instead of the other way around. She fought back tears.

"It's going to be all right," he assured her. "Your mother and I are right here if you need us. You know that."

"I know." She held on. "Can I move back in with you?"
The mantel clock ticked reassuringly in the old room, and
Katie longed for the sheltered life of her childhood again.

He held her out at arm's length to assess her expression.
"You mean leave Danny and Hardship House?"

"Yes. I can't stand either one any longer."

Her father laughed. "Come on, Katie. He'll be on the
mend soon. And you love that old bungalow."

Katie flashed her father a dubious look. "If you say so—"

℘·℘

Danny stared at the snow as it swirled against the wooden
clapboard siding and stone porch piers below, shivering under his blue blanket. The white cat appeared next to Katie's
dormant tulip bed and ran to the fence.

"There's Snowball," Danny said aloud, as his eyes followed the fuzzy white form. He watched in silence for a moment, too exhausted to traipse downstairs and peer through
the terrace doors.

A small child ran into the garden. "And there's Lily," he
whispered to himself, his heart pounding as he tossed the
blanket on the bed and hurried for the stairs. He maneuvered carefully, still lightheaded and weak despite having
completed his treatment regimen. Upon reaching the dining
room, he flung open the doors and stepped out on the patio.
He discovered the mulched tulip bed deserted. He sat in a
nearby chair and rested his head on the snow-covered table.

℘·℘

"Danny? Danny!" Katie ran out to the terrace where her
husband sat slumped over in a chair at the table.

He stirred slightly and turned his face toward her. "Oh,
hi, Katie," he mumbled.

"Come on!" She grabbed him around the shoulders. "It's
freezing out here. You've got to come inside!"

To her astonishment, Danny scooted his chair back and stood up. "All right."

The two of them walked back into the house with Katie holding onto his arm protectively. "I'll help you change your clothes," she offered, obviously shaken.

Danny nodded and remained silent.

"You'll feel much better once you're warm and dry," Katie assured him as she slipped a flannel shirt over his head.

He finished changing his clothes and then rested on the bed, unwilling to reveal why he had run out to the frigid garden and fallen asleep at the table. But Katie seemed to know. Donning a stoic look, she shook her head and turned away.

∞·∾

"We'll have to pay someone to get rid of this mold problem," Danny informed Katie from where he sat huddled under his blue blanket in his favorite chair. Winter had departed with nonstop rain, and a fungal crisis had arisen at Hardship House.

She glanced at his drawn face with reluctance. "We don't have any extra money right now."

"Well, am I supposed to just sit around in this toxic mausoleum all day? I'm beginning to wheeze."

Katie wondered if his labored breathing wasn't the result of a weakened heart—the doctor's foremost concern. "When do you see the doctor again?"

He waved her away. "Never! I'm not going back. I'm through."

It was the same every week. "Maybe you should see a psychiatrist while you're at it," she said. He'd spent half the night peering out their garden window into the rain.

"Amusing," he retorted.

"I mean it," she replied.

He studied her sardonically. "You think I'm crazy?"

"You see things that aren't there."

"The neighbors told me a white cat used to live here," Danny interjected. "Its name was Snowball."

Katie shook her head. "The previous owners didn't have any pets."

"It was before that."

"Does it come back and visit then? Is that what you're claiming?"

"Yes!"

"Well, what about the little girl?"

Danny rubbed his eyes. "A neighbor's child, perhaps... who likes cats."

Katie grimaced. The "little girl" always wore a long dress, even in the dead of winter. "I think you should at least talk to your doctor about it."

He frowned. "What does he know?"

Katie clamped down on her irritation. "Then ask someone else."

Danny held his peace. He thought for a moment of their disabled neighbor down the street. "I ought to ask him," he mumbled.

"Who?" Katie asked, certain the notion would be a nonsensical one.

"Our neighbor."

Katie knew to whom he was referring. In addition to the illusionary cat and girl, he'd developed a fascination with the injured man. "You've never even met him." Katie shook her head, feeling spent. "You need to speak to a knowledgeable therapist. I'll ask Lyndsey to suggest one."

ᚪᚱ·ᚳᚷ

Danny reclined in his chair with the morning paper resting on his chest. He felt better—well enough to read at length. He turned slightly to the left. The little girl ran into the garden in front of Katie's blooming tulip bed. He sat forward and studied the figure out the window, knowing that the moment he blinked, she'd vanish.

"Katie!" he called.

"What is it?" she replied from downstairs where she was preparing lunch.

"Look outside!" He blinked and she was gone. He heard Katie's footsteps on the stairs.

"Are you all right?" she asked from the doorway.

He appeared glum. "You should have looked. She's gone now."

Katie sighed. "Did you remember to ask the doctor about these figments of your imagination? Maybe it's from the medications you're on." He'd refused to see the therapist Lyndsey had recommended.

"It's not all in my mind. I'm absolutely sentient." He shook the paper open again. "Besides, I saw her the first week we moved into this crypt, and I wasn't on any prescriptions then."

Katie went back down the stairs, shaking her head. A mounting stack of unpaid bills lay on top of the roll top desk in her study. A pipe was leaking in the basement, but they had no money for a plumber. Danny had taped it temporarily, but it wouldn't hold for long. After her father had been so generous helping out with her final year of tuition, she dreaded the thought of asking either of their parents for additional funds.

℥·Ω

Danny waved to their neighbor and walked in his direction. The trees along the street stirred in the late afternoon breeze. He breathed deeply and listened to the rustling. For a moment, he felt strangely lightheaded.

"Everything's all right—"

Danny glanced up at the canopy of branches and grimaced as he continued across the road.

"Hello, I'm Danny, your neighbor."

The man adjusted his cane and regarded Danny with an affable expression. "Hello." He nodded and extended his hand. "Mark."

"Can I help you unload your groceries?"

"That's helpful of you. But are you sure you can manage it?"

"I'm infirm, but not dead yet."

Mark stood aside and permitted his neighbor to retrieve the groceries.

"I've been stricken with a terrific case of Lyme's," Danny continued, as he gathered up the sacks and accompanied his neighbor through the front door.

"My wife had that a few years back."

They paused for a moment inside a spacious kitchen. Danny placed the bags on the counter and turned to face him. "Really?"

"Oh, yes. We began to think she'd never mend."

"Did she?"

"Yes, she's quite well now."

"Well, I've been insufferable. My wife has been forced to work while finishing her law degree. She thinks I should see a psychiatrist because I keep seeing things that aren't there. Did your wife ever experience anything like that?"

Mark began unpacking the groceries. "What sort of things?" he inquired, ignoring Danny's question.

"A white cat... and a little girl."

"How do you know they're not there?"

"What?" Danny squinted quizzically.

"Well, if I'm not mistaken, the previous owners had your house investigated."

Danny looked surprised. "Investigated? For what?"

"Disembodied spirits. But it wasn't what they originally supposed it to be."

"Really?"

"I recall it turned out to be a phenomenon related to energy from past events trapped in some sort of time-space instant replay. Apparently the explanation resided in the realm of physics rather than the supernatural."

A small chuckle escaped Danny. "Then I'm not crazy?"

Mark smiled. "No more than any of the rest of us."

∞·∞

"What are you doing?" Katie asked her husband. He was up and dressed before dawn.

"I'm going to work," Danny replied. "Cup of coffee?"

She grew dismayed. "Did the doctor say you could go back to work?"

"I don't believe I need anyone's permission."

"Danny—"

"I'm well enough," he replied as he hurried down the stairs in his gray flannel suit.

She trailed after his lissome form, still dressed in her pajamas. "Danny—"

"How about a Cappuccino?" He reached for the machine and began preparing his drink.

"I don't think you should go."

He turned to study her, his exquisitely shaped gray-blue eyes clear under the kitchen light. "Let's just see how it goes." Oddly enough, he began to whistle.

"You're still terribly thin."

"I was born thin. Ask my mother." He pulled his nine-grain cereal from the cupboard.

Katie started back upstairs to dress. She'd prayed fervently for the day when he'd finally rouse himself from the bedroom chair and return to work. But later, as Katie watched him dash out to the car like a will-o'-the wisp in the shadowy dawn with his glowing flashlight, she felt misgivings. His blue blanket lay crumpled on the chair nearby.

Picking it up, she held it close for a moment. An unexpected realization crept into her. She already missed him.

ಏ·ಲ

"He seems to be his old self again," Katie's father remarked in an aside to Katie as they sat next to the outdoor fireplace at Hardship House. It was the Fourth of July, and Danny had just returned from a business trip out of town. He sat sprawled on top of the rockery across the patio from them, conversing with Katie's mother.

Katie heaved a long sigh of relief. "Yes, the doctor said he's going to be all right."

He placed his arm around his daughter and smiled. "Are you still planning to divorce him?"

"No." She laughed. "I guess I'll keep him."

Danny's wavy gold hair glinted under the afternoon sun as he waved to Lyndsey, who was unlatching the gate while managing a box in her arms. "Hey, Lyndsey! What've you got there?"

"A present for you."

"Me?" Danny jumped up, pleased.

A shuffling and scratching could be heard from inside the box, and Lyndsey opened the lid to reveal a white kitten. "A gotten-well present for you—" She held it up to him.

Danny cradled the tiny form close to his body. "I don't know what to say!"

"We thought you'd like her," Katie added, now standing next to them. "We picked her out at the shelter."

"We named her Snowball," Lyndsey said.

Danny laughed and stroked the furry head. "Perfect."

Katie's parents joined them. "Katie has something else to tell you, Danny. It's regarding her doctor's appointment yesterday afternoon," her mother said.

"What about it?" The date had slipped his mind in the hectic swirl of events during the past week. "Is everything all right?" He carefully handed the kitten back to Lyndsey and placed his hands on his wife's shoulders in concern.

"Just fine," Katie nodded. "We have a baby on board."

Danny clapped his hands. He covered his face and stood immobile.

"Are you all right?" Lyndsey asked, amused.

"He's fine," Katie assured her.

"Katie?"

"Yes, Danny. If it's a girl, we can name her Lily."

He nodded, peering through his fingers.

"Lily, then," Lyndsey declared, as she slapped Danny's back. "And Snowball!"

Reflections

I remember that morning clearly, as if it were only yesterday. It began like any other, with my arising early to study for school. Even though I had a year yet to go, I'd already landed a promising position where I was permitted to work part-time until I earned my degree.

When it came time for work, I put my books away, quickly dressed, and caught the eleven o'clock bus downtown. I stopped at the Garden Gate for a quick salad.

"Hiya, beautiful!" It was Mark Solinski, poised with his waiter's pad near my table. "How are you today?" He smiled down at me as if we were old pals.

"Good," I managed, trying not to make eye contact.

"You sure look great!" he replied, smiling widely while pausing for a moment to scratch his head. Tall, thin, blond, and five years older than I, he could have been attractive if he'd bothered to do anything constructive with his life. But as it stood, he was almost a comical sight, dressed neat as a pin, his gangly form sweeping around the crowded lunchroom, attempting to appease the customers. He irritated me, and I was worn out by his endless attempts to get to know me better.

"I'll have the house salad with oil and vinegar dressing," I mumbled, bracing myself. Oddly enough, he made no effort to prolong the conversation and darted away, his expression subdued. I sighed in gratitude.

After finishing my salad, I made a hasty exit before Mark could spot me and headed out into the busy town square, now mobbed with people. Checking my watch, I realized I still had a few minutes, so I stopped by the dingy fountain in the park to doze for a moment in the sun. I seated myself on the edge of a crowded park bench and stared into the dirty trickling water, observing bits of trash as they bobbed up and down in the brown foam. The treetops reflecting in the water managed to transcend the squalid little scene, however, and I watched them sway almost dreamily in the breeze.

ೞ·ೞ

I sat up with a start. Was I late for work? I glanced at my watch. It was not on my wrist.

Rising apprehensively, I stared around me in confusion. The park was gone! Instead, I stood in a clearing surrounded by trees. A creek flowing from a pool assumed the place of the grimy fountain.

I protested all of this to myself, my breath catching in my throat. Where was I? I glanced into the distance. The mountains remained, except now I could view them clearly, whereas before they had been obscured by smog. Birds trilled and whistled around me—songbirds, not pigeons. While it was still early afternoon, the place I had been no longer existed.

I must be dreaming! Yes, that was it. Having dozed off on the park bench, I was now in a dream. As a child, this had often occurred. Long ago, I had possessed the awareness while asleep to recognize when I was in a dream.

I glanced back at the pool, crystal clear and serene. Insects buzzed lazily around me. Behind me stretched a dirt road, and there was a stirring beyond the bend. Feeling somewhat reassured by my revelation that it was only a dream, I awaited something odd or inane to appear around the curve. Instead, along came a buggy pulled by a large white horse, upon which sat my younger sisters, Amy and Lisa.

"Rowena, hello!"

I stepped closer, a trifle unsure. "Hello." To my surprise, they were both clad in long dresses. Glancing down at my own form, I was startled to discover I was wearing one as well.

"Are you excited about tonight?" Lisa asked, motioning to me to climb up next to her.

I nodded automatically, studying them with interest. They appeared so different, with long shiny hair and complexions like cream.

Young Amy grew reflective. "Are you worried about something, Rowena?"

"Oh no," I assured her as Lisa gave a shake on the reins and we headed down the long, winding road. I held my peace and stared around me in astonishment and disbelief. The landscape was strangely lovely, flowing, and pastoral. How was it possible, I wondered inwardly, for my mind to conjure up a world more beautiful than any I had ever known?

Before long, a magnificent house appeared, partially hidden in a grove of spruce and hardwood trees. Lisa jumped down at an outbuilding and tended to the white horse that Amy called Sebastian.

"C'mon, Rowey!" Amy waved to me to follow her. "Let's go see what Mama's making."

Following her, I marveled that it could all seem so real. Nothing outrageous or bizarre had occurred, as it so often did in dreams. My mind was beginning to feel at ease as birds

fluttered before us and alighted in the towering trees sur-
rounding the walkway leading up to the house. Far in the
distance, I spied another graceful house along the hillside,
apparently our nearest neighbor. Amy caught me gazing at
the faraway house and smiled.

Inside we stepped into a rustic, utilitarian kitchen. "Hi,
girls." My mother embraced me warmly. Her appearance
startled me and filled me with happiness, but quickly following was a stab of sorrow. She seemed so well, rested, happy,
and in good health. "Go up and change," she advised. "Everyone will be here soon."

I trailed up a long wooden staircase to my room, admir-
ing the charm and beauty that seemed to fill every inch of
this world. I found another dress laid out on the bed and
slipped it on, combing out my long, beautiful hair with
amusement. It had been years since I'd worn my hair like
this, so wavy and full of shine.

Moments later, I was downstairs again. Voices floated
out from behind the carved double doors, and I tentatively
opened them. Inside my entire family was gathered, including aunts, uncles, cousins, nieces, and nephews. To my
shock, my recently deceased cousin was there as well, laughing and smiling, back from an early grave.

"Rowena!" they all exclaimed, obviously very pleased to
see me.

"When is he coming?" my father kidded me playfully,
sporting a beard and an easy going manner I had never
known him to have in my waking life.

"Soon!" a man who looked somehow familiar cut in,
holding up his glass to my father's. I studied him closely, but
realized I had never seen him before. "In fact, I bet he's
walking over right about now."

"I'll... I'll go meet him," I announced suddenly, the
words simply tumbling out of my mouth. With a final glance
at my late cousin, I walked back through the kitchen where

my mother and Amy were chatting while basting a large turkey.

"Is he here yet?" they both asked at once.

"Soon," I promised, as I continued on my way outdoors.

I wandered up to the fence rail where Sebastian was munching and snuffling in the green grass. I leaned against it and waited in the shadows as darkness began to fall. Far the distance, I heard whistling. Leaning forward, I felt frozen in time.

A tall figure came into view, pausing his whistling upon spotting me. With a jaunty wave, he hopped over the fence rail and, after kissing Sebastian, hurried toward me with a grin. It was Mark Solinski. He appeared healthy, vital, and in good humor.

I stared in disbelief.

"What's the matter?" he asked, growing concerned. Upon speaking the words, he began to fade... going far, far away forever, taking his perfect world with him.

I was awoken with a start by an angry shove from the man who had been sitting next to me on the park bench.

"Watch it, will ya? You're falling all over me!" Jumping up, he brushed off his arm in disgust and sauntered off.

It was all back again... the traffic fumes and yellow sky. I slumped back on the bench and closed my eyes in bewilderment, trying to recall what might have been.

৪০·ওপ্ত

Later, after work, I paused in the heart of downtown, staring at a large white horse hitched to a buggy used to carry tourists around the park.

"Hi, Rowena." Turning around, I discovered Mark Solinski seated at a bus stop nearby. "Nice horse, isn't he?"

I nodded. "Yes."

"Name's Sebastian," he informed me. Walking over to stroke the mane with affection, he kissed the old horse.

"Poor old guy, he ought to live out in the country some-place."

The public bus belched out a cloud of sooty black exhaust a block away. Mark moved back to the bench in preparation to board.

"Where are you headed?" I asked, even though it was none of my business.

He looked surprised, and then embarrassed, but stared me straight in the eyes. "To a drug rehab meeting. My last one," he announced with an expression that was serious for once. He climbed the steps of the now waiting bus and leaned for a moment, studying me intently. "How about a noon lunch with me tomorrow at the Garden Gate?" he asked. The bus driver attempted to close the doors on him, but he hung solid.

"Okay, Mark, I'll see you then."

Waving, staggering a little as the bus lurched on its way before he could be seated, Mark smiled at me through the grimy window, and I waved back.

The Lake

Untamed, formidable, and frightening… yet radiantly pure and full of light.

When she was seven years old, Katrin almost drowned just across the marina from where she now stood. That nearly fatal afternoon, she had been playing on the cliffs with her brother, Donovan, then five, while their mother busied herself indoors, packing after the divorce. His action figure doll, Lightning Man, had fallen over a precipice and down into the water below, resurfacing momentarily before floating away on its back.

Her thoughts strayed back to that long ago afternoon…

ဆ·ၸ

"Katrin! Katrin, get him!" Donovan screamed as he pointed below in a panic. Of all his action figures, Lightning Man was his favorite.

Katrin shook her head. A strange uneasiness filled her. "No, Donovan. We can't get him." Her dark hair blew across her face as she watched the doll's progress. There was no way to retrieve it, and at seven, she possessed an innate sense regarding the power of the lake that Donovan, as yet, did not have.

Her brother fell silent, his little face round like a cherub's as he studied his sister regretfully. Unlike most boys his age, he had never been prone to tantrums.

"You shouldn't have been so close to the cliff," Katrin scolded as she motioned him to follow her home. Their mother would be angry if she knew they had been playing so close to the water in the first place. "C'mon, we've got to go!"

Donovan appeared to comply, but halfway down the path, Katrin turned to find that her brother had vanished. Fear filled her.

"Donovan!" she cried out, searching behind her. Instead of running back along the footpath, however, she instinctively turned down a narrow trail that led to the lake below.

She gazed along the shoreline. Sure enough, she spotted him clinging to a fallen log in the water while he attempted to retrieve his doll.

Rushing toward him in anger, Katrin decided to hit her brother once she had safely rescued him. Before her wish could be granted, however, he fell in. She scrambled over a fallen tree and plunged into the icy water, quickly grasping him by the collar. Donovan struggled vigorously and managed to climb back up on the log. Katrin attempted to follow, but lost her footing and slipped under the swirling water.

It was the last thing she remembered about that afternoon.

છ·ૠ

Awakening some time later, she was surprised to discover herself at home in bed. The doctor and her mother stood over her.

"She'll be fine," the doctor assured her mother. He turned back to his patient with a smile. "You gave us quite a scare!"

Her mother simply stared, her expression relieved, but still somewhat ashen. Donovan stood behind them and peeked out at her guiltily, concealing something behind his back.

"It's lucky you managed to get yourself up on that shore, young lady," the doctor confided as he listened to her heartbeat for the tenth time that afternoon. It was steady and strong. "Very lucky."

The following day, Katrin gazed at her brother as their mother, who'd been fussing nervously over her children all day, presented her with a bowl of soup before leaving the room. Donovan had his back to her and was playing over in the corner by the fireplace. Observing his happy little game, she frowned and struggled to remember. Sure enough, he was playing with Lightning Man.

"Hey, how'd you get Lightning Man back?" Katrin asked, forgetting her bowl of soup. The water had dragged the doll too far out for either of them to reach. She remembered it clearly.

Her brother shrugged and refused to answer. He continued his game.

"Did he wash up?" Katrin ventured.

"Nope." Donovan shook his head. "He didn't."

"Then how'd you get him back? We didn't get him. I remember. He was too far out."

He glanced up at her warily and held the doll protectively to his chest. "Promise you won't tell anyone."

She studied her brother closely. "Okay, I promise."

"A man got him. He got you and Lightning and put you on the shore."

Katie grew incredulous, still staring at her brother. She shook her head. "There wasn't any man there."

Donovan pressed his mouth into a line, his round blue eyes determined. "Remember, you promised you wouldn't tell. He was just like Lightning Man." He examined his doll as if for the first time. "'Cept his hair was longer than Lightning's. It went way down his back. And it wasn't plastic."

Katrin exhaled in disbelief. "I don't believe you."

Strangely enough, her brother didn't seem to mind. He continued to stare pensively at the doll, his normally mischievously demeanor subdued.

"There wasn't any man there," Katrin repeated. "I didn't see him."

"That's because he came up right out of the water... like he'd been under there the whole time."

৪ও·৫3

They had moved shortly after the incident, and Katrin had returned only recently to tie up some loose ends regarding her father's estate. Turning to leave, she stared at the grandiose resort hotel that now stood where she and Donovan had once played. The water caressed her feet, and then quickly receded. With a sigh, she headed up the sand to change clothes and get ready for her appointment at the real estate office.

"I don't want the house torn down and condos put up," Katrin protested thirty minutes later to the affable man in front of her who was holding a Styrofoam cup of coffee.

"No one said they're going to put up condos. Besides, even if they did, it wouldn't detract from the beauty of the property. This developer is top notch."

Katrin hesitated. "I thought you said the offer wasn't from a developer."

He was getting frustrated with her, but made a valiant attempt to conceal his emotions. "Look, it's the best proposal we've had. That property is worth a small fortune."

She hung solid. "No, I'll wait. I don't really want it developed if I can avoid it."

He scowled and shook his head. "Well, it's your call. I was just trying to get you a good price and save you all this trouble traveling back and forth."

Katrin stood up and extended her hand. "Thank you."

ꕥ

Three weeks later, she was back again. It was nearly autumn, and the wind was whipping across the water and spraying a fine mist into the air. In the afternoon, she decided to drive north twenty-five miles to explore a historic lighthouse.

After arriving thirty minutes later, she walked along the jetty and surveyed the jagged shoreline and shimmering water, recalling that this was how the lake had appeared only a short time ago in her own town. Now the water's edge there was built up and walled in by everyone who demanded a view. The lake appeared choppy and moody as it churned against the rock wall below, and she imagined it angry over the relentless destruction of its splendor.

The wind began to blow harder and spread intermittent sheets of rain over people as they rushed back to their cars with coats pulled over their heads.

"You'd better get off the jetty. A terrible storm is coming," a man in a parka warned her. He nodded in the direction of the sloping hill in the distance where her car was parked. Katrin pulled her sweater tighter and glanced at him momentarily as he headed down to the far end of the jetty where the lighthouse stood. By the time she reached her car minutes later, she was completely drenched.

Once safely back within the confines of her late father's creaking old house, Katrin found herself unable to dispel a disquieting sensation that seemed to have no foundation. The rain was indeed building up into a horrific squall. The waves, visible out the living room window, appeared terrifying, twisting and spiraling in all directions at once. The man who'd warned her about the storm had seemed oddly familiar, yet she was unable to place his face. His hood had been pulled up, but she recalled the eyes as gray, like the tossing water.

After careful consideration, she assumed that he was most likely a lighthouse keeper she had seen in the past—perhaps in a crowd. Finally she switched off the lamp and went to sleep, the storm still raging.

The following morning, the tempest was over, and Katrin stopped by Dave's Coffee Shop and Diner for a pastry and a cup of coffee. The headline in the local paper outside on the boardwalk read: *Worst Storm of the Year Catches Community by Surprise.*

∞·∞

"Katrin, I'm afraid the quality of your work is somewhat inconsistent," her supervisor informed her, staring intently from across the room during her evaluation.

Katrin wanted to object, but realized it would be pointless. The problem with her career was that one day she did the work of three people, and the next, simply her own. Of course the quality of her work would be inconsistent. To protest the matter would be like stating the obvious.

"Also, the fact that you take time off constantly to travel up north isn't helping the situation. Have you considered possibly moving there, since you seem to like it so much?"

"No." She sighed and hoped the evaluation would be over soon. Everyone else took time off frequently, especially her supervisor, who also called in sick at least twice a month.

"Well, just sign at the bottom." The supervisor placed the piece of paper on the desk next to Katrin, disappointment emanating from her demeanor. After scanning the column of low numbers for a final time, Katrin halfheartedly scrawled her signature on the line.

"Thank you, Katrin." Her supervisor didn't smile.

Katrin turned for the door, anxious to escape. Once outside, she quickly crossed the street and headed for the little park scattered with trees. Sinking down onto a bench a moment later, she sighed again. The vocation she had once pursued so diligently was now nothing more than endless paperwork and machines with cords and wires arranged in tangles across plush carpeting. Some days, it actually seemed as though the place threatened to destroy her, but she had too many debts from her brother's legal fees to quit anytime soon.

For a moment, she considered her property up north, graced by towering trees and wild grasses, with the water glistening beyond, so unbounded and natural. The proceeds from that sale would spell an end to her financial troubles.

"Katrin, hello." A familiar face nodded her way, and she felt her heart skip a beat. He possessed such a charming smile and his expression was kind as he paused for a moment before her in the bright afternoon sunlight, holding his briefcase.

"Hello, Hadrian." She returned the smile and experienced perhaps a tiny trace of hope. It was short lived, however. A moment later, Charlene stood by his side and clasped his arm protectively.

"Hello, Katrin." Charlene managed her usual friendly concern, which didn't feel entirely genuine to Katrin.

"How is Donovan doing?" Hadrian asked, driving the stake deeper into her heart. She knew he cared about her brother, and that made the entire fiasco even more difficult to endure.

"He's doing okay," Katrin replied, disinclined to discuss the subject in front of Charlene. She had lost the district attorney's affections to Charlene forever when her brother's illegal activities had threatened to sully Hadrian's impeccable reputation.

"Well, that's good to hear." He nodded and attempted to smile again, his expression regretful. In the final analysis, there had been no way out of it for him. The responsibility had ultimately fallen on Hadrian to put her brother behind bars.

℘·℅

Katrin was up at the lake again the following weekend to review more offers from the real estate agency.

"I want the house to sell to a family," she insisted as she handed yet another offer back to the no longer so affable agent.

"That's a little unrealistic," he groused, accepting the paperwork irritably. "It's also discrimination. And you have to realize that the house is not really all that structurally sound any longer. It's highly unlikely anyone who buys the place is going to want to keep it intact."

Later that afternoon, Katrin wandered aimlessly along the shoreline, stooping occasionally to pick up bits of floating trash as she worked her way north. People crowded in around her, up for a weekend of leaf looking and fun. The water was blue today and formed tiny crests tipped with silver foam: a startlingly beautiful contrast to the brilliant fall foliage along the beach.

She squinted into the jostling crowd and froze. The man she had seen out on the jetty the night of the storm was walking through the throng just ahead of her, surveying the people around him as he passed. His hair was curly and golden brown, his stature powerful and tall. She pressed her way forward, curious to catch a glimpse of his face again. Suddenly, he turned and glanced back at her and their eyes met for an instant. She turned away self-consciously, startled by the magnetism and intelligence in his eyes.

He was gone when she looked again, swallowed up by the mob.

ଚେ·ଓଃ

That evening, she sat down to a cup of tea in the dilapidated old house, slipping into a pensive state of mind. She had cut out early from work on Friday, and the stack of unfinished paperwork lying on her desk in her office weighed on her mind. Her hasty departure was bound to land her in trouble again.

The image of the man in the crowd interrupted her thoughts about work for the tenth time that day and she sighed, her head in her hands. There was something about him that she was unable to dismiss from her mind—perhaps the expression of sincerity in his clear blue eyes when he had glanced back at her. She'd mistakenly assumed them to be gray the first time they'd met during the storm. One thing was certain: he was extraordinarily handsome, and it had been a long time since anyone had looked at her that kindly.

ଚେ·ଓଃ

It was another Tuesday afternoon. Katrin was waiting in the anteroom of the prison for her turn to talk to an inmate. Things were moving slowly today, and she'd be late for work again—another black mark on her soul. But no one in the world besides herself cared about the well-being of the young man incarcerated within these walls.

"Hi." Katrin smiled through the glass at her brother and held the phone to her ear.

"Hi." Donovan struggled to return the sentiment.

"How are you?" she asked, trying to lean as close to him as possible. They hadn't been able to touch each other for a year. Her brother appeared pale and tired.

"I'm okay," he attempted to assure her, but his eyes didn't join in with the rest of his face when he smiled. "Have you sold the house yet?" he asked, not really interested, but anxious to change the subject.

"No, not yet."

They stared at each other, a silence rising up and separating them, much like the glass that kept them apart. She had twenty minutes with him once a week, but they never seemed to have much to say to fill up the time. He was too depressed and consumed with guilt to make small talk.

"Hey, remember when you fell in the lake?" he suddenly asked, his expression losing some of its strain. "You know, right after Dad walked out on us?"

Katrin nodded. "Yes, I remember. You were trying to get Lightning Man."

Donovan laughed a little. "Lightning Man. Geez, I wonder what ever happened to him? After all that trouble, he probably ended up in a landfill someplace."

Katrin studied her brother thoughtfully for a moment. "Donovan, do you still remember the man who rescued me?"

"What?" He frowned in puzzlement.

"You told me about it the next day. You said a man pulled me out of the water."

Donovan fell silent, trying to recall the events of that long ago afternoon. "Gee, I think so. It's really hazy now, but yes, I think a man pulled you out."

"What did he look like?"

He appeared embarrassed. "I don't know, Katrin. Maybe I just imagined it all." He shook his head. "I seem to remember he looked just like Lightning Man, except he had this really long, wavy hair."

ೞ·ೞ

After the conversation with her brother, Katrin found herself wondering about the mysterious stranger of the lake. As she browsed through a bookstore one evening, she noticed a recent publication on legends and mysteries of the North Shore. She purchased a copy and read it in one sitting, finally closing the book at midnight.

Dozing off in a chair, she dreamed about the restless spirits of sailors who'd perished years ago in horrendous storms. When she awoke in the morning, she felt absolutely convinced that he was a ghost.

⁝·⁜

The next time she was in town, Katrin set her alarm early in order to watch the sun rise over the lake. Afterward, she walked back along the boardwalk, her hands nestled deep in her coat pockets and her breath making frosty little clouds in the air.

"Hello." Unbelievably, it was the hypothetical ghost. Katrin immediately regretted her ridiculous supposition and experienced a twinge of embarrassment as he smiled charmingly at her when he passed by on the walkway. "It's going to be a beautiful day today," he remarked, his expression introspective in the early morning sun.

"Really?" she asked, anxious to get a better fix on him. If nothing else, he was extremely unusual. "The weatherman said it's supposed to rain."

He laughed and waved the idea away. "No, it'll be beautiful today."

She watched him until he disappeared from sight. The sun was well up by now and it was already beginning to feel warm for so late in the year. The local news had issued a storm warning and predicted chilly temperatures and high winds.

They were wrong, however. The storm to the north swerved unexpectedly to the east. It turned out to be an extraordinarily lovely day.

ॐ·ॐ

"Katrin, I asked for that file three days ago," her supervisor admonished, glaring at Katrin from across the hall. "When do you actually plan on getting it to me?"

"Well, I'm waiting for a few more—"

"No, Katrin." Her tone was severe. "No excuses."

People in the office were eavesdropping curiously. Katrin looked away.

At her desk, she tried to concentrate, but longed to be free of the place forever. She thought of her specter up on the lake and how fortunate he seemed. After he had correctly predicted the weather, she'd decided he actually belonged to the realm of the supernatural after all. If nothing else, this supposition proved distracting and amusing, a release from the daily grind. At least someone managed to escape working for a living.

With a sigh, she pulled the file open and braced herself to do yet another substandard job.

ॐ·ॐ

She spotted him again three weeks later, the next time she was in town, seated at a bench on the pier overlooking the harbor. He was dressed in his old parka with a knit cap covering his curls, but she recognized him instantly. She paused for a moment and regarded him uncertainly, wondering once again if she were losing her sanity and simply looking at an ordinary person after all.

"You're very good at predicting the weather," she blurted out, feeling the usual rules of etiquette could be bypassed with a phantom.

He smiled and looked away. "Yes, I know the weather." He glanced back at her again. His eyes were emerald green today, like the swirling water below. That fact in itself convinced her he wasn't like anyone else. "Would you like to sit down?" He motioned to the space next to him on the bench.

"All right."

She found it difficult not to stare as she seated herself next to him. He appeared so human; in fact, much more so than other people. His humanity seemed enhanced in every way... the voice richer, the expression in the eyes deeper, the body more fit. She wondered if anyone else on the pier could see him or if he were only visible to her.

"I see you often walking next to the lake," he confided.

She nodded, enthralled by his voice. "I love the lake," she said as she studied his striking profile. "I come up here every chance I get."

"Katrin!" A friend from the city gestured to her. Two other people she recognized waved as well.

"Hello." She returned their waves, hoping they'd leave, but the group started toward her.

"I have to be going." He stood up. "Goodbye."

She grew distraught. As they approached, she wrenched her gaze away from her friends and turned back to him, but he was already gone.

80·03

The next time she visited the library, she exhausted the subject of ghosts on the Internet, particularly any sightings along the North Shore. After exiting the last website and gathering her things, Katrin felt more confused than ever. He didn't really meet any of the general criteria for ghosts—at least, not from the descriptions she'd read.

Considering the matter carefully the following week, she began down a new track in her mind and wondered if he had possibly come from another world. Perhaps he'd had to leave his own planet, come to live on this one, and had somehow assumed human form. She recalled watching a movie about that in the past. But if he had come from outer space and taken on human appearance, he had made the mistake of being a little too good at the transition. That was the most disturbing aspect of her encounters with the man: his remarkable beauty.

ᏉᏂ·ᏇᏀ

It was November, and all the leaves on the trees had fallen. Katrin continued to receive offers on the house, all of which she refused, and eventually she switched agencies.

To her dismay, Donovan informed her that he was going to be released early due to overcrowding. Despite her happiness over the news, she worried about how he would cope outside the prison walls, knowing he would have to live with her.

One weekend after a drive north of the property, she spotted the space alien on the jetty again. He stood half way down, looking out over the water. She hadn't seen him in some time and felt anxious as she approached, attempting not to appear deliberate in her actions.

It was a blustery, cold afternoon. He waved to her gallantly, all bundled up in a heavy coat.

"Hello." She returned the friendly gesture.

"Let's get out of this wind," he advised, placing his arm around her as they hurried down the jetty toward the lighthouse where they seated themselves on a sheltered bench. Protected from the wind, they rested in silence and enjoyed the view.

"I could sit here and look out at the lake forever," Katrin confided, a deep peace enveloping her. It felt timeless to look out over the water, as if her cares were forgotten. She thought for a moment of Hadrian and the possibility of never seeing him again. Unfortunately, she'd be encountering him, and also Charlene, next week at the annual employee holiday party she had helped to organize. Seeing the two of them together would make her feel as though she were drowning.

The alien stared at her with an amused smile, and she felt as though he could read her mind.

℘ · ℘

She'd hoped to see him again after the windy afternoon on the jetty, but as usual, he'd failed to materialize. The night of the holiday party, Katrin stepped out of her car in front of the building the company had rented for the festive occasion and adjusted her shawl against the cold, crisp air. She glanced at the crowd climbing the stairway that led inside. To her shock, she spotted the apparition halfway up the steps.

He waited for her. "I'm here to rescue you," he said as she approached, holding out his hand to her. She nodded, too surprised to speak.

He stayed by her side all evening, introducing himself simply as Tracy and attracting the attention of everyone in the room. Katrin was amused to see her colleagues so intrigued with something besides their careers and own importance.

Her supervisor moved closer for a better view. "Who is that man?"

Hadrian cast sidelong glances their way, his expression deeply wounded by the sight of his extraordinary replacement.

Charlene wanted answers. "Who is he?" she demanded of her friends. Suddenly it no longer felt so victorious to be seen on the arm of the district attorney.

"I bet he's one of those supermodels from Europe," a bystander ventured.

"I've never seen anyone that attractive in my life before," another woman admitted, "whoever he is."

"Thanks so much for coming tonight," Katrin told Tracy as the evening drew to a close.

"I'll get our coats, Katrin, but before we leave, I'd like you to meet a friend of mine."

He motioned toward an older gentleman across the room. She look over in surprise.

"You mean that man over there?"

He nodded, turning away to gather their things. "Yes. Why don't you say hello, and I'll be back shortly."

Katrin walked over and introduced herself. The man seemed pleased and shook her hand. After chatting a moment, he informed her that he was an attorney who specialized in environmental law.

"I live up at the lake. I'm just here with a friend."

"You've very fortunate," Katrin replied. "I love the lake. I own a property there."

"I couldn't afford to pay you what you're making here, but if you'd ever be interested in working for me, give me a call." He handed her his card.

"Thanks." She tucked it in her purse, anxious to ask him something before it was too late. "The man who accompanied me to this party tonight... he said the two of you are friends." She studied the attorney with interest. "How did you meet?"

He shook his head. "I'm afraid he's mistaken. I've never seen him before tonight. I wouldn't forget his face."

80·03

After the party, she offered Tracy a ride back to the North Shore and he accepted. On the long drive home, he remained silent. As the car rounded curve after curve in the gathering shadows, it eventually crested a hill and the lake was in view.

"Drop me here," Tracy instructed her. He pointed to a deserted stretch of shoreline.

Confused, she pulled over and switched off the ignition. They exited the car and walked to the edge of the sand where he gazed out over the dark, moving water.

"Don't do it, Katrin," he said at last. "Move into the house yourself with Donovan."

She watched him closely in the fading light. Her appointment to finalize the sale of the house was tomorrow morning. "I'd... I'd have to quit my job. Start all over again."

"You said you love the lake."

"I do."

He turned to face her. "I have to go now."

She grew anxious. "Okay, I'll move back into the house. I guess I always knew I should. Donovan and I can start a new life together."

He motioned to the sky. "I'm not from out there, Katrin."

She shook her head. "Well, who are you?"

His hair was longer and his eyes dark, like the water behind him as he looked into hers. "You won't see me like this again."

She knew he was leaving her. "Who are you?"

His shirt faded away and she saw his chest. It was covered with wounds and scars, some fresh, others old. His curls were caked with oil and trash. He was transforming to a mist before her eyes.

"I'm the lake, Katrin."

The mist floated over the water, still holding his form, then slowly descended below. Katrin watched in astonishment as he settled on the surface and she saw his face. It reflected in the water, enormous like the lake itself. The image gradually vanished, and she stood immobile as the reality of what had just happened slowly penetrated her mind.

A moment later, a gentle wave washed up and touched her foot before rolling back again.

Meet Robin

R. L. Mosz lives in Arizona. She enjoys writing and the great outdoors. To find out more, visit Robin's website at www.rlmosz.com.

Other Books R.L. Mosz

The Keeper

Roses in December

Curandero

www.ingramcontent.com/pod-product-compliance
Lightning Source LLC
Chambersburg PA
CBHW030558130626
46552CB00006B/2598